Alan Durant got the football bug at the age of eight and has never looked back. He supports Manchester United and his favourite player of all time is George Best. He has written more than forty books for children of all ages, from pre-school to teenage, and hopes one day to understand the offside rule.

Also available from Macmillan Children's Books

THE ULTIMATE FOOTBALL ACTIVITY BOOK
By Sandy Ransford

CAN WE HAVE OUR BALL BACK, PLEASE?
Football poems by Gareth Owen

BLOBHEADS
BLOBHEADS GO BOING!
By Paul Stewart and Chris Riddell

I'D RATHER BE A FOOTBALLER
Poems by Paul Cookson

Illustrated by Chris Smedley

Macmillan Children's Books

The Phantom Footballer, *Fair Play or Foul?*, *Up for the Cup* and *Spot the Ball*
first published 1998 by Macmillan Children's Books

This edition published 2006 by Macmillan Children's Books
a division of Macmillan Publishers Limited
20 New Wharf Road, London N1 9RR
Basingstoke and Oxford
Associated companies throughout the world
www.panmacmillan.com

ISBN 978-0-330-44143-8

11 13 15 17 19 18 16 14 15 10

A CIP catalogue record for this book is available from the British Library.

Printed and bound by CPI Group (UK) Ltd, Croydon, CR0 4YY

Contents

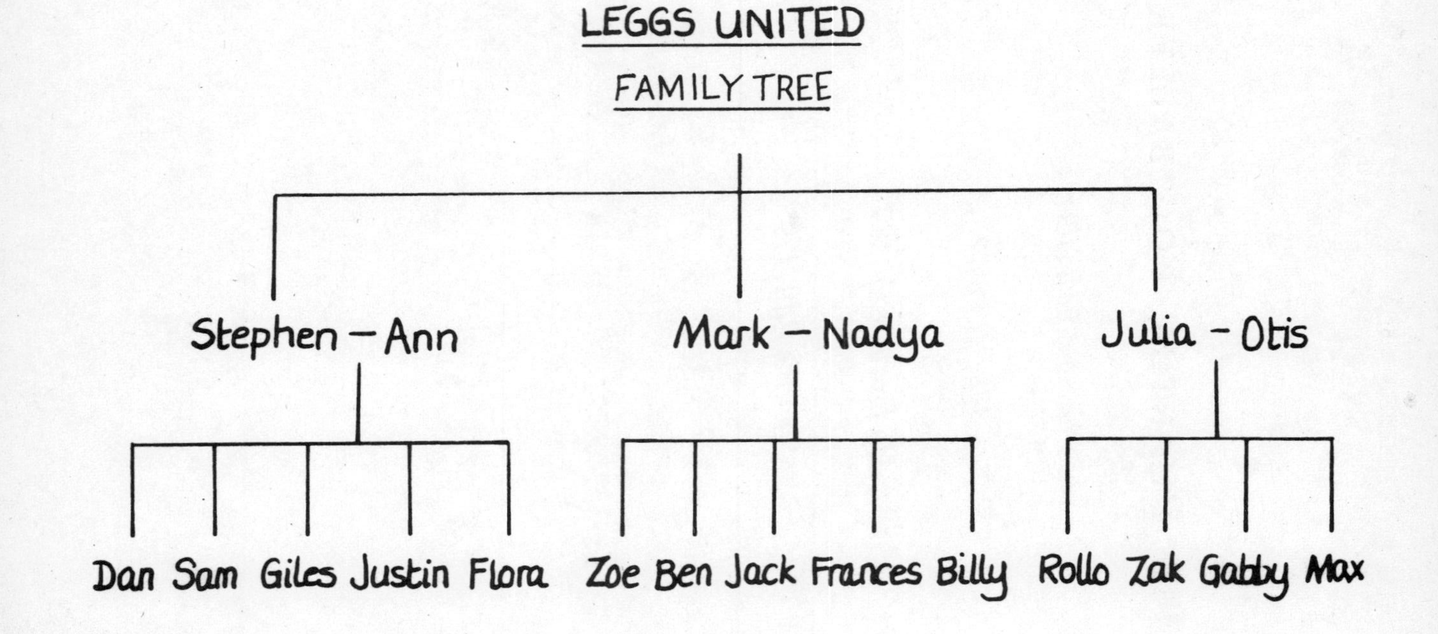
LEGGS UNITED
FAMILY TREE
Stephen – Ann
Mark – Nadya
Julia – Otis
Dan
Sam
Giles
Justin
Flora
Zoe
Ben
Jack
Frances
Billy
Rollo
Zak
Gabby
Max

The Phantom Footballer

For my own super striker,
Kit Durant

Chapter One
FOOTBALL MAD

"Goal!" Sam cried. Her powerful shot bounced against the wall, between the chalked goalposts, and back to her foot. She trapped it neatly and grinned at the goalkeeper, her brother Daniel, who was now lying on the grass in front of the wall with his feet in the air.

"Beat you there," Sam said smugly. She flicked her fringe away from her eyes. It was a warm, sunny day and her freckly face was pink from the heat.

Dan flipped himself up and shrugged. "Your turn in goal now," he said. He was ten, a year older than Sam and much bigger. He had a round face and large ears that he had a habit of tugging. Like Sam, and his younger twin brothers Justin and Giles, he was football mad. Next door there were more football-mad Leggs – their cousins. And yet more cousins, the Brownes, lived further down the street.

Sam wiped a bead of sweat from her forehead. "It's so hot," she said. "I need a drink."

She walked over to the wall that separated the meadow they were playing in from their garden. She pulled herself up.

"Good idea," said Dan. "Get me one too, will you?" He pulled at one ear thoughtfully. Even though the summer holidays had barely started, he was thinking about going back to school. This year, he'd be in the top class and in the football team. Last year, the school team had done very badly. They had let in lots of goals and lost almost every match. But this year things were going to be different. This year he would be at the centre of the team's defence . . .

There was a thump, as Sam jumped down

from the wall into the meadow. A bottle of orange drink wobbled in front of Dan's eyes.

"Your drink, master," said Sam.

"Oh, thanks," said Dan. He took the bottle and drank deeply. Then he burped loudly.

"Ah," he sighed contentedly, lying back on the grass. "I was thinking about next year," he said, "playing for the school team."

Sam humphed. "It's not fair," she grumbled. "I'm as good as you. I should be in the team too." She sat down on the grass next to her brother.

Dan laughed. "That's the rule," he said. At Muddington Primary only children in the top year could play for the school football team. "Anyway, who says you're as good as me?" he demanded.

"I do," Sam replied. It was a typical Sam remark. She wasn't big-headed, she just always said what she thought.

"Well, then, if you're so good, get in that goal and prove it," said Dan.

Sam wrinkled her snub nose. "I didn't say I was good in goal," she said. "I'm better than you at scoring, though."

"And I'm better at tackling," said Dan.

"Oh, *tackling*," said Sam, like she didn't think tackling was very important. She loved to run and dribble and shoot like her hero, Tommy Banks, Muddington Rovers' striker and top goalscorer. She wasn't interested in *tackling*.

"Defenders have to be good at tackling," said Dan.

"Strikers don't," Sam replied. "They just have to score."

As if to prove the point, she jumped up and whacked the ball against the wall again. The ball bounced back and hit Dan on the back of the head.

"Oi!" he cried. He sat up suddenly as if he'd been stung by a bee. "Careful!" His pink face went even pinker.

Luckily for Sam, at that moment the twins appeared, peering over the wall. They were dressed in identical T-shirts and baseball caps. Their faces too were identical and wore the same excited expression.

"Hey, Dan! Sam!" they called as one.

"Mum and Dad are clearing out the loft!"

Justin cried. "There's some great stuff!"

"They've even found an old football," Giles added. "Come and see!"

As soon as they heard the word "football", Dan and Sam were on their feet. They pulled themselves up and over the wall. Then they raced across the garden towards the house.

Chapter Two
THE OLD BALL

There was junk everywhere – in the hall, up the stairs, draped over the banisters. Some of it was neatly packed away in cardboard boxes and black plastic sacks. Lots more lay about in untidy heaps. Number 15 Poplar Street, where Sam and Dan lived, had been a Legg house for generations. Their dad, Stephen Legg, and his brother, Mark, and sister, Julia, had all grown up in it. Some of the stuff in the loft had been there since before they were born!

As the four siblings reached the landing, a

shower of baby clothes dropped on to them from above. They shouted and, looking up, saw the big bearded face of Stephen Legg beaming down at them.

"Oh, sorry about that," he said with a chuckle. He blew out his cheeks and wiped his forehead with one large, grubby hand. "This is hard work," he declared. "My arms are aching something rotten. Is there a doctor in the house?"

"Of course there is," Dan said. "You."

Stephen Legg frowned momentarily as if he'd forgotten. Then he grinned. "Oh, yes, so I am," he said.

"Where's the ball, Dad?" Sam asked impatiently. "We've come to see the ball."

"Yes, show us the ball!" cried the twins, who often said exactly the same thing at exactly the same time.

"Ah, yes, hold on a sec," said Stephen Legg. He vanished for a few moments then, "Catch!" he called. An object dropped out of the loft and Dan caught it.

"Is that *it*?" he said. It didn't look much like a ball. It was brown and squashy like a

baseball mitt and sort of boat shaped. It had a big dent in the middle with a lace in it.

"That's not a *ball*!" Sam groaned.

"Of course it is!" cried their dad. "It's a good old-fashioned leather ball. It's just gone flat, that's all. So would you if you'd been lying in that loft for over fifty years! All it needs is pumping up and maybe rubbing with some dubbin to bring the bloom back to its cheeks."

"Balls don't have cheeks!" protested Justin and Giles.

"What's dubbin?" asked Dan. He was still staring at the ball as if it was a piece of old junk that should be thrown in the bin.

"It's a kind of polish," said Dad. "It's just the thing to put the life back into old leather. You'll find some down in the shed. You could pump some air in the ball while you're there."

Dan looked hard at the ball. Then he looked at his dad. He seemed serious enough. "OK, then," he said. "Come on, Sam."

The shed was a big concrete hut at the bottom of the garden. It was full of bikes and tools, pots and cans and all sorts of stuff. Dan got a pump and the special valve to screw on to it, while Sam looked for the dubbin.

There was a whole shelf of different cans and plastic containers: linseed oil, varnish, wood glue, white spirit . . . She searched along the row, until, at last, she found the dubbin.

"Got it!" she cried.

"Good," said Dan. He'd pushed the

needle-like valve into a hole under the lace in the ball and now he started to pump. *Clunk, hiss! Clunk, hiss!*

Sam looked at the tin of dubbin. *For making leather soft and waterproof,* it said on the lid. She opened the tin and stared at the bright apricot-coloured stuff inside. She touched it with her finger and sniffed. It didn't really smell much.

"Look, it's going up!" Dan puffed. Slowly, the ball's shape was changing. The dent was rising. After a while, the ball was full and round. Dan bounced it on the floor and then gave it a kick.

"Ow!" he said, shaking his foot. "That hurt."

Sam felt the ball too. "It's really heavy," she said. "I wouldn't like to head that."

"Not without a crash helmet," said Dan.

Now that the ball was pumped up, they could see just how worn and scuffed the leather was.

"You'd better put some of that stuff on," Dan said, nodding at the dubbin. "You can use this." He threw Sam an old cloth.

Sam took the cloth and scooped some dubbin out of the tin. Then she started rubbing it on to the ball. The leather went a little bit darker. She did the same again, rubbing harder now. She was dipping the cloth in the tin for a third time, when the shed door opened and their cousin Zak Browne came in.

"Hi," he said pleasantly. "What are you doing?" He was the same age as Dan and they were best friends.

"I'm putting dubbin on this old ball that

Dad found in the loft," Sam said, rubbing another dollop into the leather.

"Cool," said Zak, pushing back a black ringlet of hair from his eyes.

"Dad says this ball's over fifty years old," Dan said.

"Wow!" said Zak.

Sam rubbed more dubbin into the old leather, which had started to shine a little now. She wrinkled her freckly nose. "I feel like Aladdin," she said. She rubbed some more. "Arise, O genie," she moaned in a high, quivery voice that made Zak and Dan laugh. "Arise, O genie of the ball."

And then it happened. There was a sudden blaze of light, and out of the ball appeared a ghostly figure . . .

Chapter Three

ENTER ARCHIE

Sam dropped the ball and jumped back, while Dan and Zak stood stock-still, staring in amazement at the shimmering figure before them.

It was a man with bright red hair that stood up on his head like a shock of flames. He had big bushy eyebrows and a huge walrus moustache. It was difficult to say exactly how old or how big he was, because he was sort of fuzzy and glimmered at the edges. He was dressed in a football kit in the colours of Muddington Rovers: a black and green striped shirt, white shorts and green socks.

But it was a Muddington Rovers kit from long ago. The shirt had a collar and no name or words on it; the shorts were baggy and long. He wore big shin-pads under his socks and his boots were clumpy with steel toe-caps. Between the bottom of his shorts and the top of his socks two bony knees showed, so pale you could almost see through them. Round his neck, the figure wore a red knotted handkerchief like a cowboy.

"Wow!" said Sam shakily.

"Wh-who are you?" whispered Dan.

The phantom footballer stood with his hands on his hips and one foot on the old ball. In the gloomy light of the shed, he seemed to glow. He eyed the children keenly.

"Well, let us get one thing clear from the kick-off," he said sharply. "I am *not* a genie!" He waggled his moustache. "Genius, perhaps." He smiled proudly. "My name is Archibald Legg. I *was* the inside-right and star player of Muddington Rovers. I am *now*, for my sins, a ghost."

"A ghost?" Dan repeated.

"A ghost!" Sam exclaimed.

"Cool," said Zak.

Sam frowned. "But . . . there's no such thing as ghosts," she said.

Archibald Legg drew himself up and glared at Sam. His eyes appeared to fizz.

"Look, here, laddy," he said fiercely. "I have been squashed inside a flat football for goodness knows how long, waiting for somebody to release me. Now, at last, I am free and you say I do not exist. I tell you I am a ghost as surely as you are a boy."

His face flickered and he raised his eyebrows in a challenging look.

"But I'm not a boy," said Sam. "I'm a girl."

Archibald Legg peered at Sam again. "Of course you are, of course you are," he muttered. "It was just a figure of speech. The point is, I *am* a ghost and I *am* here. Now, *who are you*?"

"I'm Sam," said Sam. "Sam Legg."

"I'm Dan, her brother," said Dan.

"I'm their cousin, Zak Browne," said Zak.

Archibald Legg appeared a little confused.

"His mum's our dad's sister," Dan explained.

"Ah," sighed Archibald Legg. "Do you know, it's lovely to be amongst family." His thick eyebrows parted like two woolly caterpillars going their separate ways. Then he smiled so that his moustache stretched amazingly. "Now that we have been properly introduced," he said cheerfully, "you may call me Archie. Everyone does."

"Pleased to meet you, Archie," said Sam.

"Yeah," Dan agreed with a big grin.

"Cool," said Zak, who was still totally awestruck by Archie.

Archie nodded happily. "I wonder, are there any more of you Legg and Browne lads?" he enquired.

"Oh, yes, lots," said Dan. He did some quick mental maths. "Fourteen," he added. "But we're not all lads."

"Mmm," said Archie. He stroked his moustache thoughtfully. "A whole team, eh, and more?" he mused. "I should like to meet them all," he announced. Then he yawned. "But right now, I think I shall take a little nap. Daylight is very tiring, you know, when you haven't been in it for so long." His eyes blinked woozily and he seemed to slip out of focus. "What is the date, by the way?" he asked wearily.

Dan's reply had a dramatic effect. Archie's eyes almost popped out of his head and his hair stood up even more. He quickly faded. Within seconds, he had vanished into the ball, as if sucked through the valve hole beneath the lace.

The three children looked at the ball in

astonished silence, half expecting their phantom visitor to reappear. But he didn't.

"Shall we call him back?" said Sam at last.

"He said he needed to rest," said Zak.

"Yeah," Dan agreed. He moved forward and picked up the ball. "Come on," he said excitedly. "Let's go and tell the others."

Chapter Four

IT'S MAGIC!

Ann and Stephen Legg were still busy in the loft. They were looking for things to sell on the stall Ann Legg was going to run at the following Saturday's Muddington House Summer Fair.

"Mum! Dad!" Dan called, racing up the stairs with Sam and Zak behind him. "Come down. We've got something amazing to show you."

Ann Legg's hot, red face appeared at the loft opening. "Can I sell it on my stall for lots of money?" she puffed.

"No," Dan cried. "It's much too special for

that." He held up the ball. "This old ball's magic," he said.

Breathlessly, Dan and Sam told their mum about the ball and about Archie. She looked doubtful.

"Archie says he wants to meet you all," Dan babbled.

"He does, he does!" Sam shouted.

Zak nodded his head in a storm of black ringlets. "It's true, Aunty Ann," he confirmed.

"You've got to come down and see," Dan appealed. His large ears were scarlet with excitement. "*Please.*"

"Well, perhaps we should have a tea break," Ann Legg said wearily.

"Put the kettle on, Dan," said Stephen Legg.

"OK!" Dan cried. Then he, Sam and Zak tore off downstairs again.

"Mad, completely mad," sighed Ann Legg, shaking a clump of dust and fluff from her dark hair.

"It runs in the family," said Stephen Legg, as the twins burst past him and hurtled down the loft ladder.

*

"You know, that ball *might* be worth something," said Ann Legg, sitting on the sofa, nursing a mug of tea. "Perhaps we *should* sell it on my stall."

"No way, Mum!" Dan cried in horror.

"It's you who'll benefit, you know," Ann remarked sharply. The money raised from the stall was going to Muddington Primary, where most of the Legg children were pupils and where Zak's mum, Julia Browne, was a teacher.

"You can't sell it, Mum," Sam said indignantly. "It's *magic.*"

"Yeah," Zak agreed. "There's a ghost in it."

"Well, that would certainly put the price up," Stephen Legg teased. "Perhaps we could sell it to Holt Nolan to present to the winners of his Football Challenge."

Holt Nolan, a rich local businessman, was the owner of Muddington House. Every summer he held a fair in its grounds at which he ran a mini football competition. Muddington Colts, the junior football team that he managed, challenged any team to try to beat them. So far, no team ever had: the Colts always won.

It was generally believed that Holt Nolan only held the competition as an opportunity to show off his team and to present the fancy silver trophy to his elder son, George, who was the Colts' captain. His younger son, Perry, played for the team too. He was Dan's arch-enemy at school.

Dan grasped the old ball to his chest tightly. "No way is Perry getting this ball," he said grimly. His parents smiled.

"Don't worry, Dan," said Stephen Legg gently. "No one's going to take away your ball."

"No," Ann Legg agreed. "But what about this magic business?"

"Yeah!" the twins chorused. "Do some magic, Dan!"

"I want magic! I want magic!" chanted Dan's little sister, Flora, and everyone laughed.

Dan waited until they were all quiet again. "We aren't joking, you know," he said very seriously. "This ball really is magic." He told them again about Archie's sudden and shocking appearance and the conversation that had followed.

"Now you can all meet him," he said. He looked down at the old leather ball in his hands. "Archie," he said softly. "Archie, come and meet your relatives."

Nothing happened.

"Come on, Archie," he pleaded. "They're dying to meet you. Really they are."

Still there were no ghostly stirrings . . .

"It doesn't look like Archie's dying to meet us," said Ann Legg drily.

"Well, if he's a ghost, he'll be dead already, I suppose," Stephen Legg remarked.

"Dad!" said Dan sternly. "You're not taking this seriously. Archie really is . . ." He hesitated an instant. What *was* Archie? A ghost? But that sounded silly, didn't it? "Archie is real," he said finally.

"Yeah," said Sam.

"He's cool," Zak added. He glanced across at Dan. "Maybe Sam should do what she did before," he suggested. "You know, that Aladdin stuff."

Dan pulled at one ear and frowned. "OK," he shrugged. He handed the ball to Sam, who started to rub the ball gently.

"Arise, O Archie," she commanded in the same quivery voice she had used in the shed earlier.

Everyone laughed again. The twins fell against each other giggling.

"Arise, O Archie," Sam wailed once more and she rubbed the ball a little harder.

And this time, just like a genie from a magic lamp, Archie did indeed appear.

Chapter Five

ARCHIE AGAIN

Archie's second appearance was even more dramatic than his first – he came fizzing out of the ball like a firecracker. He looked more ghostly this time too. He was fuzzier at the edges and quite transparent in places.

For an instant or two there was total shocked silence as all eyes focused on the shimmering figure. Then the room erupted with voices crying out, shrieking, screaming. Flora hid her head in her mum's lap. Stephen Legg's mouth gaped open with amazement. The twins jumped up and banged heads. Dan and Sam threw up their hands in excitement. Only Zak remained calm.

It was a while before order was restored. Then Archie had to face an explosion of questions. Who was he? Was he really a ghost? How long had he been in the old ball? Was it true he was related to them? If so, how? Archie met all these questions with an indulgent smile. He stroked his big red moustache carefully, as if making sure each individual hair was in place. Then he raised a commanding hand.

"Listen and I shall tell you my story," he said. He put his hands on his hips and waited for silence before continuing. "My name, as I have already told these young lads here," – he glanced with a smile at Dan, Sam and Zak – "is Archibald Legg and I believe I am indeed related to all of you in this room. I was born in 1905 and died . . . well, er, in 1938, I believe. So, yes, I am a ghost. When I was alive, I played for Muddington Rovers and, though I say it myself, I was rather good. The great Herbert Chapman, when manager of

Huddersfield Town, once offered £150 for my services."

"£150!" Dan exclaimed and he laughed. "Alan Shearer cost £15 million."

"£15 million for a football player!" Archie was horrified. "In my day you could buy every player in the world for that amount of money." His eyes glinted and gleamed with outrage.

"He's a very good player," Sam said gently.

"I dare say he is," said Archie. He pushed out his chest a little. "So was I."

"What happened to you?" Dan asked. "I mean, how did you die?"

"Ah," sighed Archie. "I was the victim of a cruel catastrophe!" His thick eyebrows joined in a bushy frown. "One stormy day, in the winter of 1938, I was playing in a cup match for Muddington Rovers against Newcastle when suddenly, out of the blue – well, the black actually – a bolt of lightning hurtled from the sky and struck me down, just as I was about to score. I was killed immediately."

At this terrible memory, Archie flickered with emotion. He looked down gravely at the

old football. "This ball was the match ball that day and I have been trapped inside it ever since. I cannot tell you how delighted I am that you rescued me. I had no desire to spend the whole of my ghostly existence inhabiting a pig's bladder."

"A pig's bladder!" cried the twins, Giles and Justin, and they squealed with laughter.

"The inside of an old football, the bit you pumped the air into, used to be made from a pig's bladder," Stephen Legg explained.

"Gross," said Sam.

"Yeah," Dan agreed.

"So you've been up in the loft, inside that ball, all these years?" asked Ann Legg incredulously.

Archie nodded his large head. "Indeed I have," he said. "While the ball was dead, so was I. But when these kind children revived it, I too was revived." He gave Dan, Sam and Zak a gracious nod. "And here I am, back in the bosom of my family."

"Now, let me see," mused Stephen Legg, "judging by when you were born, you must be my grandfather's brother. My *great*-uncle." His face flushed with excitement. "Of course, Great-Uncle Archie!" he cried. "I remember my grandfather talking about you. We must have a photograph of you somewhere."

"So you're the children's great-great-uncle," Ann Legg reflected.

"Cool," said Zak.

Archie positively glowed with pleasure. "Well, now that I'm here," he said happily, "I intend to make myself useful. I couldn't help overhearing some talk of a football challenge.

That wouldn't be the Football Association Challenge Trophy you were talking about, would it?" he enquired hopefully.

"Eh?" said Dan.

"He means the FA Cup," laughed Stephen Legg. Then, turning back to Archie, he added, "We were talking about the Holt Nolan Football Challenge." He explained to Archie what this was.

"Oh, I see," said Archie with some disappointment. "Well, every team must start somewhere."

"But what team?" said Dan. "We don't have a team."

"Well, there are enough of you to make a team, aren't there, laddy?" said Archie sharply. "How many did you say you were? Fourteen, was it?"

"Yes, but . . ." Dan stammered

"You only need eleven players to form a team," Archie persisted. "At least that was the case in my day . . ." His eyes blazed, challenging anyone to contradict him. "Well then, what better than to have a family team?" he declared triumphantly. "Leggs

Eleven, I shall call it." He waggled his huge moustache thoughtfully. "Or Leggs United, perhaps?"

Stephen Legg studied his ancestor shrewdly. "Are you suggesting that the children form their own football team to play the Muddington Colts in the Holt Nolan Football Challenge?" he asked.

Archie nodded once vigorously, his shock of red hair flickering like fire. "Indeed I am," he confirmed.

"What a good idea," said Stephen Legg with a big grin.

"Call it ghostly inspiration," said Archie smugly.

"But the Muddington Colts are nearly all eleven or twelve," Sam protested. She thought briefly. "Only Dan, Zak, Rollo and Zoe are over ten."

Archie tutted at her. "Age is no matter in football, laddy," he said. Then, before Sam could correct him, he continued, "It's talent that counts – and expert management, of course." He stared at Sam, Dan and Zak with narrowed eyes. "And you will have a manager of unrivalled skill, experience and tactical genius."

"We will?" said Zak.

"You will," said Archie.

"Who?" asked Dan with a bewildered frown.

Archie puffed out his chest and raised his thick, red eyebrows. "Why, me, of course," he said with pride.

Chapter Six

ARCHIE GETS ELECTRIC

The next afternoon, Archie held his first training session in the meadow at the bottom of the gardens of number 15 and number 17 Poplar Street. The meadow belonged to the Legg family and was the size of a large football pitch.

Sam summoned Archie from the old football and, as on each previous occasion, his appearance caused great excitement. Most of the cousins had only seen Archie once, when he had been introduced to them all the evening before, so they still found him quite astonishing. By contrast, Dan, Sam and

Zak were very calm. It was weird, Dan thought, how quickly you could get used to having a ghost in the family.

"Now, before we commence training," Archie said importantly, "you had better tell me your names again."

"I'm Dan," said Dan with a grin.

"Yes, I know you," said Archie. "And Zak and Sam – and Miles and Julian . . ."

"*Giles* and *Justin*!" shrieked the twins together.

"Oh, yes, of course, of course," said Archie fuzzily.

One by one the other members of the newly formed Leggs United introduced themselves: Rollo and Gabby Browne, Zak's brother and sister; then Zoe Legg and the triplets, Ben, Jack and Frances, and their little brother Billy. He was a bit young for the team, but Archie said he could join in the training.

"He can be our super sub," said Dan.

"Super sub?" queried Archie.

"Yes," said Dan. "Our substitute. In case anyone gets injured."

"Substitutes aren't allowed," said Archie sternly.

"Yes they are," said Sam. "You're allowed three."

"Three!" cried Archie. "In my day, if someone got injured you played on with ten men. That was part of the excitement." He shook his head in disbelief. "You'll be telling me next that players can be substituted because they're not playing well enough."

"Yes, they can," said Sam.

"Huh," Archie snorted. Then he tutted with disapproval. "What would the great Herbert Chapman make of that?" His eyes narrowed to two hairy lines. "Well, there's no *substitute* for hard work," he declared sharply. "So let's commence training. We'll start with some keep-ups." He looked keenly at the group of children before him. "Now, which of you lads is going to kick off ?"

"I will," said Sam quickly.

Archie glared at her, his bushy eyebrows bristling. "In my day," he said, "girls played hockey and netball. They did not play football."

"I do," Sam said defiantly. "And so do my cousins."

Archie studied Sam and Zoe in their Muddington Rovers shirts and Gabby in her goalkeeper's jersey. "You have the clothing," he said. "But can you play?"

"Of course we can," said Sam fiercely.

"They can," Zak said. "They're really good." He nodded at Sam. "Show him your keep-ups, Sam," he urged.

Sam nodded. She flicked a football up in the air and kicked it. She trapped it on her knee and kicked it up again. She kicked the ball with her left foot up in the air, over and over again. In all, she did twenty-five keep-ups.

"Mmm, not bad," Archie said. He stroked his big red moustache appreciatively. Then he turned to Dan, who was smiling broadly at his sister's feats. "Now, laddy," said Archie. "You show the girls how it's really done."

Dan's smile quickly vanished. "What?" he spluttered. "Me?" His ears went bright red.

Archie nodded.

"But I'm a defender," said Dan.

"Well, defenders play football, don't they?" said Archie.

"Well, yes," said Dan doubtfully.

"Go on, then," Archie insisted.

Reluctantly, Dan took the ball. He did five keep-ups. Then he stepped on the ball, lost his footing and fell flat on his face. The other children laughed.

"Mmm," Archie uttered. "Not very impressive."

Dan got to his feet gingerly. Then he picked up the ball. He held it out to Archie. "You show us," he challenged.

Archie raised one eyebrow. "Well, it has been a long time," he said. "Toss the ball up, then . . ."

Dan threw the ball in the air. As it fell, Archie stuck out his right foot casually to catch it. But the ball carried on dropping, right through his foot, and bounced on the grass beneath.

Archie's eyes and mouth opened wide with astonishment. His eyebrows hopped alarmingly. "Oh, er, well," he said. He tried to kick the ball with his other foot. But the same thing happened. Archie scratched his head and peered down in dismay at his booted foot and then at the ball.

"It appears that I am lacking in substance," he remarked mournfully. He looked so upset that Dan felt sorry for him.

"Maybe you just need to do some exercise," he suggested helpfully. "You know, to build up your strength, after all those years inside a ball."

"Your energy level is probably low," said Zak thoughtfully. His favourite TV programme was *The X Files* and he knew quite a lot about ghosts and the supernatural. "I saw this programme the other night about ghosts and electricity," he continued. "When a ghost is near electricity it gets more energy and its body gets more, well, solid – like ours."

"Maybe Archie should put his finger in an electric socket," said Sam.

Archie frowned. "I've already been electrocuted once, thank you," he rasped. "I have no desire to repeat the experience."

Zak shook his head. "No," he said. "It's more a question of trying to draw the waves of electricity in from around you, I think. You know, think electric."

"Think electric?" Archie queried, his big moustache twitching. "I don't understand what you mean."

"I get it!" said Dan excitedly. He pointed to a garden nearby where a man was cutting his grass. "See that electric lawnmower, Archie," he said. "Think of the power that's surging through it. Try and draw some of that power into your body."

Archie still looked completely bemused, but he did as Dan suggested. For about thirty seconds, he stared at the lawnmower with deep concentration. Then he sighed. "I cannot feel a thing," he said sadly.

"Try again," Zak urged. "Really concentrate."

"Go on, Archie!" the twins chorused as one.

Once more, Archie focused on the lawnmower. He stood completely silent, eyes staring, head and body completely still – and the children stood still and silent too, watching him.

For several seconds, nothing happened. Then, all of a sudden, there was a hiss and a fizz and Archie's shock of red hair seemed to blaze from his head. The faint glimmer that surrounded him became a dazzling light: Archie quivered and shone.

When he turned to face the children again, his face was beaming.

"I feel as if lightning has struck for a second

time," he announced happily. "But this time it's brought me to life."

He aimed a kick at the old football. It zipped away through the air and thudded against the wall, scaring a fat crow that was sitting there.

"Now," Archie declared, "that is more like it."

Chapter Seven
GHOSTLY GOALIE

Over the next few days, Archie spent a lot of time practising drawing electricity into his body – with increasing success. His energy levels shot up amazingly. He became a ghostly dynamo and worked his team very hard. Every morning they had a long training session that started with a run around the meadow and ended with a short six-a-side game.

In between, Archie taught the children a variety of skills. He showed them how to dribble and bodyswerve, how to nutmeg and sell a dummy, how to volley and bend a shot like a banana. They practised trapping the ball, passing, shielding, tackling and, of course, keep-ups.

"You must learn to be the ball's master and not the reverse," Archie told his players. "As the great Herbert Chapman once said, 'Control the ball and you control the match.'"

Archie mentioned Herbert Chapman a lot and always with deep respect. In Archie's opinion, Herbert Chapman was the greatest manager that had ever lived. He won the championship twice in a row with Huddersfield Town and was on the verge of achieving the same feat with Arsenal when he died, suddenly, of pneumonia.

Recalling his hero's death, Archie shimmered with emotion. He actually looked for an instant as if he might burst into tears. His moustache quivered and his eyebrows trembled. Then he took a deep breath and steadied himself.

"Right, on with the training," he commanded. "Ball skills. Dan, toss a ball up."

Just as he had a few days before, Dan threw

a ball in the air. Once again, as the ball dropped, Archie stuck out his right foot to catch it. The children watched, breath held, wondering what would happen . . .

This time the ball landed on Archie's foot and stayed there. He held it for a moment then, with a contented smile, he flicked the ball up again and caught it on his left foot. He juggled the ball from foot to foot, then from knee to bony knee. Then he bounced the ball on his head, eventually letting it roll down his back and over his bottom. When it reached his calf he kicked up his heel and flicked the ball back over his head and into his hands.

"Wow!" said Dan.

"Cool," said Zak.

"Do it again!" demanded the twins. So Archie did. This time he balanced the ball on top of his head, before allowing it to slide down his back. When he'd finished, everyone clapped.

Archie glowed so much that his hair looked as if it was on fire. "Thank you, thank you. You're too kind," he said happily.

The children were constantly amazed by

Archie's football skills. It seemed as if he could do anything. He could even play in goal. Gabby was the Leggs United goalie. She wasn't very tall but she was a very good gymnast and had an amazing spring. After Thursday's training session, Archie gave her some extra coaching. Dan, Sam and Zak stayed behind to watch. Archie showed Gabby how to come out and narrow the angle when faced with an attacker, where to stand for corners, and lots of other useful tips.

"I'll tell you a little goalkeeper's trick," he said with a theatrical wink, as if he were passing on some priceless secret. "When I played in goal, I used to make a little mark at the centre of the six-yard line to help me get my positioning right."

"Were you a goalkeeper then?" Gabby asked, puzzled. "I thought you were a forward."

"Ah, yes, indeed I was," said Archie. "But I often took a turn in goal in practice matches and on a few occasions, when our goalkeeper was injured, I was called upon to take his place." He smiled smugly. "I was rather good, too," he declared, "though I say it myself." The cousins raised their eyes and groaned.

As if to prove the point, Archie went in goal and invited Dan, Sam and Zak to take shots at him.

The ghostly goalie proved quite impossible to beat. He leapt and dived in a fiery flash that took him from side to side, up and down. He saved everything.

"How do you do that?" Dan marvelled, as Archie plucked yet another goalbound shot from the air.

"Yeah, that was cool," Zak agreed.

"Call it phantom power," Archie replied mysteriously, tapping his long nose with a bony finger.

Gabby looked rather disheartened. "I'll never be as good as you," she said flatly, her shoulders drooping.

"Nonsense, nonsense," Archie retorted quickly with a waggle of his huge moustache. "You'll be just fine. I've not seen such an agile young keeper since the great Frank Swift was a lad." This compliment was met by bemused silence.

"Who's Frank Swift?" Sam asked at last.

"Who's Frank Swift?" Archie repeated incredulously. "Who's Frank Swift? Why, only the best goalkeeper of his age." He threw up his large hands dramatically. "Indeed, of any age, I should venture," he added.

"What, better than you?" said Dan mischievously.

Archie grinned broadly. "Well, let's say he was one of the two best keepers of his age," he said.

Chapter Eight

THE INVISIBLE MANAGER

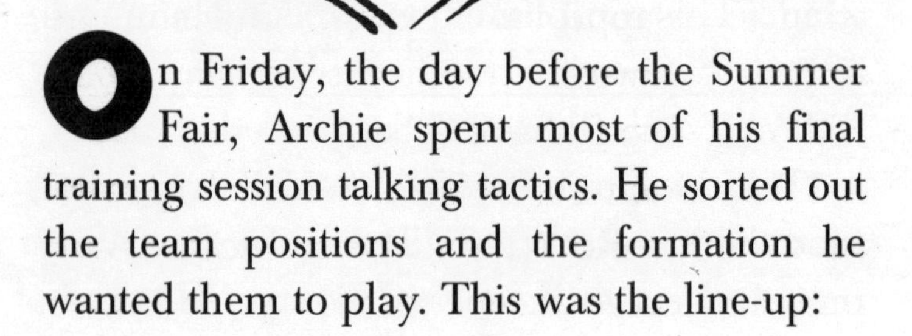

On Friday, the day before the Summer Fair, Archie spent most of his final training session talking tactics. He sorted out the team positions and the formation he wanted them to play. This was the line-up:

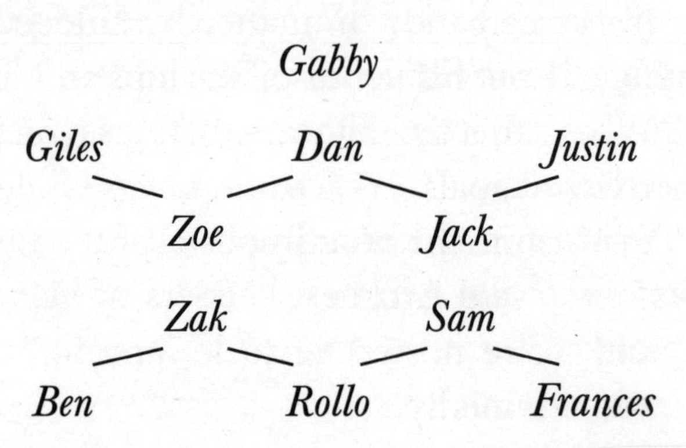

"Is that 3-2-2-3?" asked Dan.

"I suppose you could say so," said Archie. "It was Herbert Chapman's invention, the WM formation. It made Arsenal the greatest team in the world." He gazed upwards with an odd, dreamy look. "Hulme, Bastin, Lambert, Jack and James – what a forward line."

"Muddington Rovers play 3-5-2," said Sam.

Archie's expression turned from admiration to disapproval. "Do they indeed?" he sniffed. "However do they score any goals with only two forwards?"

"They don't very often," said Zak glumly. Muddington Rovers had been relegated the season before.

"Well, there you are, then," said Archie huffily. He put his hands on his hips and fixed his team with a fizzing stare. "*We* are going to score lots of goals, are we not, Leggs United?"

"Yes!" came the unanimous reply.

"Good," said Archie.

"And we're not going to let any in," said Dan determinedly.

"I should think not," agreed Archie. "Not with you at the heart of our defence." He paused a moment before continuing, with a nod at Gabby, "And with young Frank Swift there in goal, of course."

Gabby smiled. "I'll do my best," she said eagerly.

"That's all anyone can do," said Archie. "It's the spirit that counts." He stroked his moustache proudly and put one foot on the old ball. "And when that spirit is Archibald Legg," he declared, "the opposition had better beware!"

At that moment, as if on cue, a horn blared, announcing the arrival of Perry and George Nolan. They were on their bikes, looking over the wall across the meadow. As the assembled Leggs and Brownes turned round, Perry sounded his horn once more.

"Up the Colts!" he cried.

Dan greeted his enemy with a hostile scowl. "What do you want?" he called fiercely.

"We just stopped by to size up the opposition," said George, smirking.

"Yeah, we heard you're entering the Challenge tomorrow," said Perry. He jerked his head at Dan and sneered. "We'll thrash you," he boasted.

"Says who?" Dan replied.

"Says anyone with half a brain," George goaded.

"Hear that, Archie?" said Dan, turning to his manager, who was still standing with one foot on the old ball.

"Indeed, I did," Archie replied coolly. "Take no notice. We'll do our talking on the field of play."

"What's that, then – your lucky mascot?" Perry said, nodding at the old ball.

"Archie!" scoffed George. "Funny name for a ball." The two brothers sniggered.

"He wasn't talking to the ball, you idiots," Sam hissed. "He was talking to our manager, Archie. He used to play for Muddington Rovers."

Archie raised his head and smiled smugly.

"I don't see anyone," said Perry, looking around with a baffled expression.

"Yeah, where is he then, this Archie?" demanded George.

"There, you wallies," said Dan, pointing at Archie.

"What are you talking about?" said George. "There's no one there – just an old ball."

Dan frowned and tugged at his ear. He was the one looking baffled now.

"You can't see Archie?" he said. "He's standing right there with his foot on the ball."

"You're nuts," said Perry. "There's no one there." He studied the Leggs contemptuously.

Then his face suddenly screwed up in disgust. "You've got girls in your team!" he cried.

"You really will need a lucky mascot," laughed George. "Come on, Perry," he said, "let's go and tell the others the good news. Leggs United are rubbish. And they're bonkers!"

"Yeah," said Perry. The two got back on their bikes and turned to go.

"See you Saturday, suckers!" shouted Perry as the brothers cycled away.

For a few moments, there was silence in the meadow. Then Dan said quietly, "They couldn't see you, Archie."

"It seems not," Archie agreed, frowning sadly.

There was another moment's silence, then Zak spoke up. "Maybe only your relatives can see you," he suggested.

"What do you mean?" asked Dan.

"That happens sometimes with ghosts," said Zack. "I read about it in a book."

Archie pondered this idea with a slow caress of his moustache. "Well, as long as *you* can see me, I suppose that is all that matters," he said at last. He looked in the direction the Nolan brothers had taken. "They'll see my genius in action soon enough . . ."

Chapter Nine
SURPRISE SURPRISE

On Saturday morning, Dan was woken by an excited Sam. She was hopping up and down at his bedside, shouting something about a surprise. "Come downstairs!" she cried. "Come and see!"

Dan yawned and rubbed his eyes. Then he rolled out of bed and shuffled downstairs after his sister. "What is it?" he asked sleepily.

And then he saw. His eyes popped open. Suddenly he was wide awake.

"Wow!" he uttered. In front of him stood Sam and the twins, each wearing a smart new football shirt, with red and white squares and the words *Legg's Motors* across the front. Behind the children, holding up an identical shirt, was their uncle Mark.

"How do you like your new team strip, Dan?" he asked, passing Dan the shirt in his hands. Dan stared at the new shirt, then he looked at his sister and brothers.

"It's brilliant," he said.

"Look at the back," said Sam. Dan turned the shirt round. On the back was a black number 5 and his name.

"Cool," he said, delighted. He pulled the shirt on over his pyjama top and then ran off to look at himself in the mirror. The others followed him.

"Thanks, Uncle Mark," Dan said, when he'd finally finished admiring himself. "It's really great."

"Well, you can't be a proper team without a proper kit, can you?" Mark Legg shrugged. "Besides, it's good advertising for my garage." He grinned and touched the silver ring in his ear. "Well, as long as you win, of course."

"Don't worry, we'll win," said Dan airily.

Later, however, when they got to the fair, he didn't feel quite so confident. Holt Nolan's Football Challenge had already begun. Two other teams, besides Leggs United, had entered. Each game was to last 40 minutes; 20 minutes each way. In the first game the Colts had thrashed their opponents ten–nil, and they were now playing – and easily beating – the second team.

Dan and the rest of his team arrived just as Perry Nolan scored to give the Colts a 4–1 lead. The goal was a simple tap-in, but the way Perry celebrated, you'd have thought it had been something really spectacular. He leapt in the air and shouted, then dived across the pitch like an Olympic swimmer.

"Show-off," Daniel tutted. "Wait till he's facing me. I'll show him."

"Careful, though," said Zak. "Don't forget, his dad's the ref." He nodded across at Holt Nolan, who was standing in the middle of the pitch with a whistle round his neck and a smile about ten metres wide.

Dan humphed. "Like father, like son," he said grimly. Then he looked down at the old ball he was cradling in his arms. "I think it's time we called Archie," he said.

Archie was a little confused at first. He looked fuzzier than ever; almost as if he'd been sketched on the air with a blunt pencil, Dan thought. He glanced about, checking to see if anyone had noticed the phantom footballer's arrival. No one had. Several people walked by without batting an eyelid. It seemed, then, that what Zak had suggested was true: Archie was only visible to his family.

"Where am I?" Archie asked groggily. "What is all this?" He peered around blearily at all the people and the stalls, at one of which the adult Leggs were now busy selling their wares. "Is this Wembley Stadium?"

"You're at the Muddington House Summer Fair," Sam informed him.

"For the Holt Nolan Football Challenge," Zak added.

"We're on next," said Dan. He gestured to where the Muddington Colts were celebrating yet another goal. The game was almost over now and there was no doubt who was going to win.

"Ah, yes, of course, of course, the Challenge," Archie muttered. "When you woke me I was playing in the Cup Final. I'd just scored a wonderful goal. Frank Swift never had a chance." He grinned hazily at the memory.

"Do ghosts have dreams then?" Dan asked. It seemed an odd idea to him.

"Of course we do," snorted Archie. "It would be a dull old life if we didn't." His moustache wiggled, as if something was not quite right. "Well, a dull old death, if you see what I mean," he added.

He looked around at his players, glowing with proud satisfaction as he took in their smart new strip. "Right, there's no time to lose. I'll just get myself charged up and then we shall have our final team talk . . ." He started focusing on a generator which was powering a nearby bouncy castle.

A few minutes later, as Archie and Dan were talking about corner tactics, two opposition players joined the Leggs on the touchline. It was Perry and George Nolan, fresh from their recent victory.

"Still talking to that old ball?" Perry jeered. "Oh, sorry, I mean your manager." He turned to George and they both sniggered.

"Just ignore them," said Archie calmly. "Stay cool."

"You'll be laughing on the other side of your face when we beat you," said Dan defiantly.

"You've got no chance," Perry scoffed. "My dad's offered to donate £500 to Muddington Primary if we lose."

"So?" said Dan.

"Dad never gives away money to anyone," said George with a knowing grin.

"*And* he's the ref," Perry added, smirking.

George Nolan gave the magic ball a rude prod with his foot. "Hello, anyone in there?"

Archie could take no more. His calm ignited into fury. He hopped up and down and shouted, "Hoodlum! Whippersnapper!" He gave the Nolan brothers such a fiery glare that some of the younger Leggs shrank back in alarm. But not George and Perry Nolan. After all, they couldn't see or hear Archie, could they?

"See you on the pitch," said Perry casually.

"Yeah, for the slaughter," added George. Then the two brothers walked away, sneering.

Now Archie was really fuming. He waved his fist at the departing Colts. "Mock Archibald Legg, would you?" he snarled. Then he turned to face his team with an expression of wild determination. "Right, Leggs United," he declared. "This is war!"

Chapter Ten
ARCHIE EXPLODES

The match started well for Leggs United; after just two minutes, they took the lead. Dan booted the ball upfield; Sam trapped it neatly on her chest and flicked a pass across to Zak. Taking the ball in his stride, Zak swerved past George Nolan and lashed the ball into the net.

The Colts looked stunned. After their two easy wins, this wasn't at all what they'd expected. Reluctantly, Holt Nolan blew his whistle and pointed back to the centre. Then he gave his oldest son a severe telling-off for letting Zak get past him.

On the touchline, the adult Leggs clapped and cheered.

"Great goal, team!" shouted Stephen Legg.

"Let's have another," Mark Legg added.

"Nice one, son," called Zak's dad, Otis Browne, giving a thumbs-up sign.

Archie hardly moved a muscle. He stood quite still with his arms folded, one foot on the magic ball, as if posing for a photo. His face bore a look of calm contentment. Everything appeared to be going perfectly to plan.

It didn't last long, however. Less than a minute later, Leggs United were in trouble. Perry Nolan's striking partner, Matt Blake, ran between Jack and Justin and then knocked the ball through Dan's legs as he came across to tackle. Gabby came out to narrow the angle, as Archie had shown her, but Matt was too quick. He flicked the ball past her towards the goal. It was just about to roll over the line and into the net, when Perry raced forward and threw himself at the ball, so that he could claim the goal for himself. Once again, he celebrated like he'd scored the goal of the season.

Dan felt sick. He was cross with himself for falling for Matt's nutmeg trick and fed up that it was Perry who'd scored. But worse was soon to follow. In their next attack, the Colts got a corner kick and Rollo headed the ball into his own goal. From being a goal up, Leggs United were 2–1 down!

For the rest of the first half, the Colts were well on top. The ball was hardly out of the Leggs' half. Archie's tactic of booting the ball down the wings for Frances and Ben to chase just wasn't working. Both were very fast runners for their age, but they were up against defenders who were three years older than them. Only Gabby's brilliant goal-keeping and some timely tackles by Dan kept Leggs United in the match.

It was no surprise when the Colts scored a third goal. It came after one of Leggs United's rare attacks. In the excitement of finally getting the ball into their opponents' penalty area, Zoe and Jack rushed upfield to support the front five players. As one, the twins went chasing after them. When the attack came to nothing and the Colts' goalie booted the ball clear, only Dan was left in defence against both Perry Nolan and Matt Blake.

The ball ran to Perry, but he didn't trap it cleanly. Seeing his chance, Dan moved across and tackled his enemy. It was a good tackle but, unluckily for Dan, the ball bounced away off Perry's shin straight into the path of Matt Blake.

Once again, Gabby came out to narrow the angle. This time, she managed to get a hand

to Matt's shot, but she couldn't stop it going into the net. 3–1 to the Colts!

Archie's cool turned to rage. As the Colts celebrated, he burst onto the pitch like a wild fire. His target was Holt Nolan.

"Offside!" he exploded at the referee, his face red with fury. "Are you blind, you fool? Don't you know the rules? That was offside by a mile!"

The Leggs players and supporters turned and stared in astonishment at Archie, who was now waving his fists at Holt Nolan. It looked as if he was about to punch him on the nose.

"Archie!" Stephen Legg cried. "What are you doing? Get off the pitch."

Archie turned and glowered at his relative. "It was offside," Archie repeated angrily. "Didn't you see?"

"The rules have changed, Archie," Zak explained soothingly. "Matt was standing in line with Dan. That's not offside now. Really. It was a fair goal."

Archie greeted this information with a thunderous scowl, but he did leave the pitch.

He gave Holt Nolan a scorching glare, growled something under his breath and then marched back to the touchline. His outline pulsed with rage.

Holt Nolan, meanwhile, had trotted back to the centre and the Muddington Colts had lined up for the kick-off. A few of them pointed at Zak and shook their heads in amusement. As far as they could see, he was explaining the rules of football to thin air!

Holt Nolan peeped his whistle. "Are you still in this game, Leggs United?" he shouted impatiently.

"Come on, Leggs United!" Mark Legg urged from the touchline.

The Leggs players turned and gaped at one another uncertainly. They hadn't moved since Archie's outburst and looked as if they were in a dream, awaiting their manager's instructions. But Archie was too busy fuming to give any orders. It was up to the captain, Dan, to wake his team up. He clapped his hands sharply.

"Let's go, team!" he cried. Then he ran back to take up his place in defence.

"Doesn't look like your lucky ball's working," Perry sneered as Dan jogged past him.

"The game's not over yet," Dan flung back defiantly.

But in his heart, he feared it might be.

Chapter Eleven
A CHANGE OF TACTICS

Half-time came at last. The score was still 3–1 to the Colts, but only because Perry Nolan missed an open goal. Just a couple of metres out, with Gabby on the ground, Perry decided to blast the ball when all he had to do was tap it over the line. The ball thundered against the post and rebounded straight into his stomach, knocking him flat. He writhed around and groaned like a snake with bellyache. Holt Nolan blew his whistle.

"Half-time," he called, running over to his felled son.

Normally Dan would have laughed at

Perry's antics, but not now. He trooped off the pitch, glumly, with the rest of the Leggs.

"Well tried, team," Stephen Legg said encouragingly.

"Yes, there's still another half to go," Mark Legg pointed out.

"Hmm," Dan uttered gloomily. Another half like the one they'd just had wasn't much to look forward to. What would Archie say about what had happened?

As it turned out, Archie was now surprisingly calm and at ease. He'd cooled down once more and was sitting on the old ball, stroking his moustache thoughtfully.

"I see things are a little different from in my day," he reflected. His eyebrows hopped critically. "Not better, certainly not, but different. A few tactical changes are in order, I believe."

The main problem, Archie said, was that the defence and attack were too far apart. The long ball over the top of the Colts' defence wasn't working at all and the front W was playing too flat. The system needed tweaking. So, while Zak's mum, Julia Browne, handed round drinks to the team, Archie made some tactical changes.

For the second half, Leggs United would line up with the same WM formation, but now Jack and Rollo would play in front of the defence, with Sam and Zoe pairing up behind the forwards Zak, Frances and Ben.

The new arrangement would look like this:

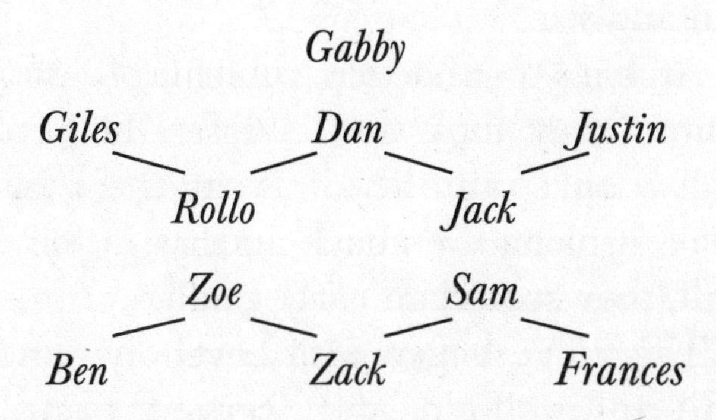

"You two are the linkmen," Archie told Sam and Zoe. "You have to link defence and attack – the role I often played myself for Muddington Rovers." He smiled proudly.

"Link *girls*, you mean," said Sam, frowning indignantly from under her fringe.

Archie's smile became a steely glare. "You may be girls," he said sternly, "but I expect you to play like men. The success of our attacks depends upon you."

"Huh," Sam snorted. "We'll show you how we can play."

Archie told Dan to stay close to Matt Blake and not allow him any room on the ball. "Stop him and you stop the Colts," he declared with a flamboyant waggle of his moustache. "It's as simple as that. Now, go out and win!"

Archie's confidence rubbed off on his team. They took the field for the second half with spirits lifted. From the whistle, they went on the attack and, as in the first half, they scored an early goal.

The move began with Sam. She got the ball in midfield and weaved past two defenders before sliding the ball down the wing. For once, Ben had lots of space and no defender near him. He raced along the wing to the goal line and sent over a teasing cross. The goalkeeper stretched but could only push the ball into the path of Zak, who slammed it into the net. 3–2 and Leggs United were back in the match!

As Leggs United found new energy, the Colts began to tire. This was, after all, their third game of the day. Perry Nolan was puffing and panting, while Matt Blake couldn't get away from Dan at all. For about the tenth time in the half, Dan took the ball off the Colts' striker and fed it through to Rollo. On it went to Zoe. She was tackled by George Nolan but the ball ran to Sam. A quick sprint forward, a swerving shot, and the ball was in the Colts' net for the equalizer.

"Great goal, Sam!" shouted the adult Leggs, applauding heartily.

Sam glanced across at Archie. "Not bad for a girl, eh?" she called.

Archie raised his hairy eyebrows and nodded with approval. He was the picture of contentment once more.

It seemed only a matter of time now before Leggs United would score again – with Sam really enjoying her playmaking role and Zak a constant threat upfront. The Muddington Colts looked dead on their feet. The game was all being played in their half.

But the goal wouldn't come. Zak went

close twice, Ben hit a post and then Sam had a goal disallowed by Holt Nolan for offside.

"No way!" she cried, furious at the decision.

"The referee's decision is final," said Holt Nolan smugly.

"Hey, stay cool," Zak told Sam. "We'll get another chance."

He was right. With just minutes left, Leggs United finally got the breakthrough their play deserved. George Nolan hit a weak back pass. Quick as a flash, Zak ran on to it, flicked the ball past the goalie and banged the ball into the net. There was nothing Holt Nolan could do this time, except blow his whistle to signal a goal. Zak had his hat-trick and Leggs United were in the lead!

Now Archie did get excited. He leapt up and did a little jig, his bony white knees pumping up and down in a ghostly whirr. Dan laughed. The spectating Leggs cheered. Like Archie, they thought the game was all over. But the Nolan family had other ideas.

A last desperate clearance from the Colts bounced deep into the Leggs United half. Perry Nolan chased after it. Dan made no attempt to follow. It was a hopeless chase because Gabby was going to beat Perry to the ball quite easily. Still Perry carried on running. The ball rolled into Gabby's arms. She collected it and stood up – just as Perry arrived. He ran right up to her and threw himself to the ground as if he'd been tripped. It was the most outrageous dive Dan had ever seen. No referee could fall for that, surely?

But then Holt Nolan wasn't just the referee, was he? He was also the manager of Muddington Colts and Perry's dad too. He blew his whistle at once.

"Penalty kick!" he cried and, to everyone's disbelief, he pointed to the spot.

Chapter Twelve

ARCHIE LENDS A FOOT

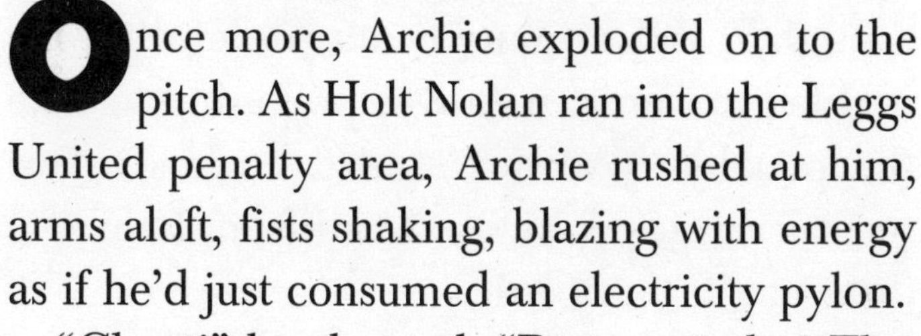

Once more, Archie exploded on to the pitch. As Holt Nolan ran into the Leggs United penalty area, Archie rushed at him, arms aloft, fists shaking, blazing with energy as if he'd just consumed an electricity pylon.

"Cheat!" he shouted. "Dirty swizzler! This is the most disgraceful refereeing display since that fool Harper ruined the 1932 Cup Final!"

Holt Nolan might not have been able to see or hear Archie, but he could feel him. Archie shoved him and sent him stumbling backwards. The Colts' manager cried out in surprise and looked down at his chest, where Archie's hands had touched him. Then he glanced about with a baffled expression.

After a moment or two, he shrugged and, collecting himself, strode forward again, straight past Archie, who was still pulsing with anger.

"It's amazing," Dan said to Zak. "The Colts *still* can't see Archie, even when he's glowing like that."

"They can see the ball and the goal, though," Zak pointed out dolefully. He nodded at Perry, who was preparing to take the penalty. "We don't need a ghost – we need a miracle," he muttered from behind a drooping mop of hair.

"Gabby might save the penalty," Dan said hopefully, pulling nervously on one ear. He didn't really feel very hopeful. His cousin was a good goalie, but she wasn't used to facing penalty kicks. Perry practised taking them a lot. He was always boasting about how good he was at penalties. If he scored, the game would end in a draw and that meant that the Colts, as champions, would keep the Challenge Trophy.

But Archie had not given up. While the Leggs United players lined up dejectedly at the edge of the penalty area, he bustled into the goal beside Gabby. He studied Perry Nolan for an instant with a keen eye.

"Feint to go left, then dive to your right," he instructed.

"How do you know he'll shoot that way?" Gabby asked.

"Call it ghost's intuition," Archie replied

mysteriously. He stepped back behind the goal line, arms folded.

Gabby shrugged. "OK," she said. She swayed from side to side, getting ready to face Perry's kick.

Perry grinned triumphantly at the Leggs United players, most of whom had their heads down, unable to watch. But not Dan. He glared back at his enemy defiantly. The whistle blew. Perry raced forward and thumped the ball towards the corner of the net.

As soon as he'd hit the ball, he leapt in the air, certain he'd sent Gabby the wrong way. In fact, he'd already spun around to receive his team-mates' congratulations when Gabby reached the ball and pushed it past her right-hand post.

Now it was the Leggs' turn to celebrate. They shouted and jumped in the air and hugged one another. Off the pitch, the adults did the same. Dan ran over to Gabby and they slapped hands in a high five.

"David Seaman, eat your heart out," Dan said excitedly.

Still standing behind the goal line, Archie grinned like a manager who'd just pulled off a master stroke. "Frank Swift could not have done better," he remarked happily.

A blast of Holt Nolan's whistle brought the Leggs United's celebrations to a sudden end. "The goalkeeper moved before the kick," Holt Nolan declared. "The penalty must be retaken."

Dan stared at the referee in total astonishment. "What?" he cried.

Zak, who knew the rules inside out, quickly came to his friend's support. "But that rule changed in 1997," he protested. "She's allowed to move, as long as she stays on her line."

Holt Nolan shook his head. "Don't argue with the referee, sonny," he said. "That's the oldest rule in the book." Then before Zak could comment, he went on, "The kick's got to be retaken and that's final. This is my competition and you do what I say."

Archie met this latest injustice with glowering contempt.

"So that's the way you want to play it, sir,

is it?" he growled. Then he ordered everyone except Gabby out of the penalty area.

"There is no use in arguing with this petty chiseller," he said. "Do as he says."

"What about me?" Gabby asked. "Which way should I go this time?"

Archie pursed his lips. "Neither way," he said. "Stay exactly where you are."

"But if he puts it to either side, he'll score," Gabby said.

"Trust me. Don't move," Archie insisted. He tapped his long nose. "We ghosts know about these things." He closed his eyes and frowned as if in deep concentration.

Once again, the ball was put on the penalty spot. Holt Nolan blew his whistle. Perry sprinted forward and kicked the ball. This time, though, he kicked the ground as well and scuffed his shot. The ball rolled towards the line, nearer to the centre of the goal than the corner. All Gabby had to do to make a save was take a few steps to her right. But she didn't. She stood right where she was, just as Archie had commanded her. Dan watched, helpless and horrified, with the rest of his team, as the ball trickled towards the goal line . . .

"Move, Gabby!" squealed the twins. "Move!"

But Gabby didn't move – and anyway now it was too late. The ball was about to cross the line. It was a certain goal.

There are two different views as to what happened next. In the eyes of Holt Nolan and his team, an incredible, freak event occurred: as the ball reached the goal line, it hit a hidden bump and changed direction, bobbling away from the goal and round the post.

What the Leggs United players and supporters saw was quite different. They saw the ball roll towards the line and the steel toe cap of an old boot shoot out to flick it away. They even saw the huge grin on the phantom footballer's face after he made the save.

Whichever view you choose to accept, the result was the same. The penalty was missed and Leggs United had won!

Chapter Thirteen

SWEET DREAMS

"We won the cup, we won the cup, ee-aye-addio, we won the cup!"

It was Saturday evening and Sam was dancing round the kitchen, singing, with Holt Nolan's Football Challenge Trophy on her head. She was still dressed in her Leggs United strip.

"Hey, watch out you don't drop it," said Dan, with an anxious tug of his ear. He still couldn't quite believe that the trophy was theirs, that they'd actually beaten the Muddington Colts. It was just too amazing. He smiled as he recalled the sour look on

George and Perry Nolan's faces when he walked forward to collect the trophy. Their dad looked pretty sick too. But then they deserved to feel bad. "Cheats never prosper," as Stephen Legg had remarked on the way home.

It had been a great day for the Legg family. Leggs United had won the Holt Nolan Trophy and Ann Legg's stall had been a big success and raised lots of money for Muddington Primary. Moreover, Holt Nolan had had to donate £500 to the school. He had not been happy.

"It was brilliant, wasn't it?" Sam said now, her freckly face bright with happiness. She plonked down on to a chair, her fringe flopping over her eyes, and put the trophy onto the table next to the old ball.

"Yeah," Dan sighed. "It was."

He gazed lovingly at the trophy for a minute or so, then he turned his gaze to the old ball. A week ago it had lain flat and forgotten in the loft with Archie trapped inside it. So much had happened in the days since then, he thought, that it was

impossible now to imagine life without Archie.

"Let's call Archie," Dan said. "I'd like to thank him."

Sam nodded. "We couldn't have done it without Archie," she agreed. She leant forward and picked up the old ball. Then rubbing it gently, she began the familiar wail.

"Arise, O Archie," she chanted. "Archie, arise."

An instant later, Archie fizzed out in front of them, glowing gently in the murky evening light. Dan took in once again the shock of red hair, wild eyebrows, huge walrus moustache, the old Muddington Rovers football strip with long, baggy shorts, bulky shinpads and heavy boots, the bandy legs and white, almost transparent kneecaps, the knotted neckerchief . . .

"We just wanted to thank you," Dan greeted his ghostly relative. "On behalf of the whole team."

"Yes, thanks, Archie," Sam said. "You're the best manager in the whole world."

Archie's pale, shimmering face coloured a little and his moustache wrinkled. "Thank you, thank you. You're not so bad yourself," he said good-humouredly. "For a girl."

"Cheers," Sam said with a big grin.

"Thanks for the helping foot too," said Dan. "We needed that."

"Yes," said Sam. "You were truly electric."

"Foot? What foot?" Archie queried, all innocence. "The ball hit a bobble. Wasn't that the referee's official verdict?" His face screwed up into an expression of deep distaste. "I cannot abide cheats," he hissed.

"That game was won fair and square."

"Yeah, it was never a penalty," said Sam.

"Indeed, it wasn't," Archie said. "That's why I did what I did. It was a matter of justice." His expression relaxed into a blissful sigh. "Anyway," he continued, "I believe my tactical genius bamboozled them."

"Those tactical changes certainly worked a treat," said Dan.

"Yes," agreed Archie. "The WM formation may have its critics, but to me it is proof of Herbert Chapman's genius. Next time, I'm sure, we shall get it right from the start."

Dan frowned. "Next time?" he enquired. "What next time?"

"Next time you play," said Archie casually.

"When's that, then?" asked Sam, intrigued.

"In a short while, when the new season commences," Archie informed them. "Your father has agreed to enter you in a local league. The same one, I believe, that the Muddington Colts play in." His eyebrows rose artfully.

"Wow," said Dan.

"Great!" cried Sam.

"Indeed," said Archie. "And now, I must return to my pig's bladder to repose. It's been a very tiring week for an old ghost." He yawned. "Tomorrow we can commence planning for the great challenge ahead." He raised a large, bony hand in farewell. "Goodnight, sweet dreams," he muttered. And with these words, the tired but triumphant Leggs United manager began to fade, dematerializing into the old ball.

"Goodnight, Archie," said Dan. "Sleep tight."

"Watch out the bugs don't bite," Sam added warmly.

Then the two children stood in silence, staring at the faint glow in the air left by the phantom footballer, until it had vanished entirely.

Fair Play or Foul?

For my toughest tackler,
Amy Durant,
with big love

Chapter One

SOFT AS BUTTER

"Ow!" Dan cried, hopping up and down in pain.

"Sorry, mate," said the Downside attacker who'd just kicked him on the shin. "I was going for the ball."

Dan grimaced and rubbed his sore leg. "Going for the ball!" he exclaimed. "You weren't even close." He shook his head in disgust.

"Are you OK, Dan?" asked Giles, one of Dan's younger twin brothers. "Is your leg broken?"

"You look really white," said Justin, the other twin.

"Like a ghost," Giles added.

"Yeah, like Archie," Justin confirmed. At the mention of their ghostly relative, the twins glanced across at the touchline.

The late Archibald Legg, former inside forward and star of Muddington Rovers, now the phantom manager of Leggs United, was in his usual match pose. He stood very straight with his hands on his hips, one foot on the old ball which, for over sixty years, had been his home. He was dressed, as ever, in an ancient Muddington Rovers strip with thick shin-pads and clumpy leather football boots. The paleness of his skin contrasted with the bright red of his big caterpillar eyebrows, enormous walrus moustache and fiery shock of hair. Around him there was a strange ghostly shimmer that blurred his outline.

At this particular moment Archie's face bore a hugely contented smile. Leggs United, the team he had formed during the summer from the children of three related families – two sets of Leggs and their cousins, the Brownes – were 3–1 up in their opening game of the season. It was also their first match ever in the Muddington

Junior League, a local football league for under-twelves.

Archie couldn't have hoped for a better start. His tactics had worked to perfection. The Leggs United score could easily have been doubled if the post and the bar hadn't come to Downside's rescue. As it was, goals by Sam, Zak and Ben had put Leggs United in a comfortable position. Downside's goal had been no more than a late consolation.

The full-time whistle blew and Archie nodded with satisfaction.

"Well played, team," he congratulated his players as they walked off the pitch. Dan was the last to leave, hobbling behind his younger sister Sam and his cousin and best friend Zak Browne.

"Well done, laddy," Archie greeted him. "You played a true captain's part."

"Yes, and I've got the bruises to show for it," Dan grumbled. His round face bore a pained expression.

"A few bruises never hurt," declared Archie, his moustache bristling. "Why, I often used to finish a match black and blue. It's a man's game, you know."

Sam humphed indignantly and flicked her fringe back.

"Well, you know what I mean," Archie added hastily. "Of course," he continued, "football was tougher in my day. The ball was much heavier and the boots were a lot harder." He glanced down at his own polished steel toecaps. "If you got a kick on the ankle from one of those you knew it all right. Why, I remember . . ."

Archie was fond of talking. After spending over half a century in Dan and Sam's loft, trapped inside an old football with no one to talk to, he was eager to make up for lost time. From the moment he'd fizzed out of the old ball like a genie from a magic lamp, he'd made a huge impression on his young relatives. He loved telling them what football was like in his day and, most of the time, they loved to listen. Right now, though, Dan wasn't in the mood for listening to stories. He just wanted to go inside and rest his bad leg, then go home and lie in a nice, hot bath. When Archie paused for an instant, he quickly seized his opportunity.

"Mum and Dad are waiting. I think we'd better go and get changed," he said. "Come on, Sam, Zak."

He picked up the old ball and started limping away.

"Soft as butter," tutted Archie and he raised his bushy eyebrows dismissively. Then, his ghostly size-twelve boots hovering above the ground, the phantom footballer glided across the grass towards the changing rooms.

Chapter Two
LEGS AND NO LEGS

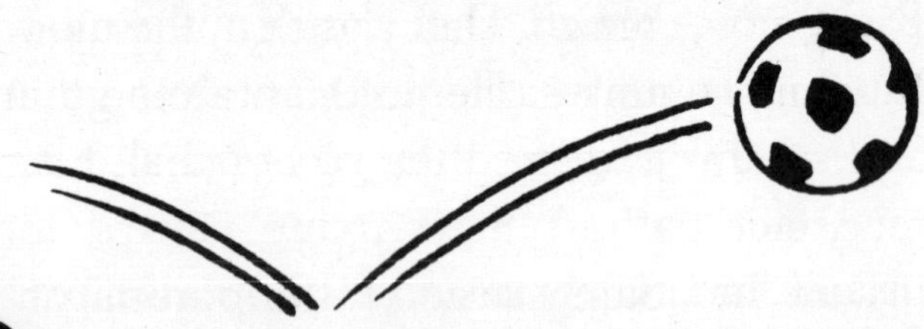

Dan's leg was still sore next morning. There was a big brown and yellow bruise on his shin. He showed it to Sam at breakfast.

"Eugh," she said. "It looks like a mouldy banana."

"Sounds nasty," said their dad, Dr Stephen Legg, pouring himself a cup of tea. He peered at Dan's leg. "You ought to wear shin-pads, you know."

"I will in future," said Dan ruefully.

Sam pulled a face. "I don't like shin-pads," she said. "They slow you down and they're uncomfortable."

Stephen Legg laughed and shook his head. "You think they're uncomfortable *nowadays*," he said. He went over to the kitchen dresser, opened one of the doors and took something out. "Take a look at these," he said. "I found them in a junk shop the other day."

Ann Legg looked up from her newspaper. "Not more junk," she sighed. It was while clearing out junk earlier in the summer, that the Leggs had discovered the old football haunted by Archie.

Dan and Sam stared at the objects on the table in front of them.

"What are they, Dad?" Sam asked.

Dan picked up one of the objects and studied it. It was shaped a bit like a cowboy's gun holster. The front was made of grooved leather, the kind he had sometimes seen on the seats of old cars in Legg's Motors, his uncle Mark's garage. The back was flat and stiff. The thing itself was quite thick, though, so it must have been stuffed with something. It was surprisingly heavy too.

"Is it an old shin-pad?" Dan said at last, pulling at one of his ears.

"It is," his dad confirmed with a nod of his large, bearded face. "Imagine playing with those under your socks. They'd slow you down all right."

"These must be like the ones Archie wore when he played," Dan said. "No wonder he didn't care about getting kicked. I reckon you'd break your toe if you kicked one of these."

"Yeah," Sam agreed. She screwed up her freckly nose. "How could anyone play football in those?"

"Why don't you ask Archie?" suggested Stephen Legg.

"Good idea," said Dan. "Come on, Sam." He picked up the old shin-pads and they went off into the sitting room to call up Archie from the old football.

The ball was now kept in a glass-fronted cabinet, on top of which was a framed photograph of Archie in his playing days, before he'd been struck down by a bolt of lightning. Dan gazed at the photo while Sam took the ball out of the cabinet and started to rub it gently. Then, as if she were Aladdin summoning the genie, she wailed, "Archie. Arise, O Archie!"

Barely a second later, Archie was there. He leapt out of the ball in a quivery fizz and loomed over the children, shimmering. It was a dramatic entrance, but Dan and Sam hardly batted an eyelid. They were used to Archie now.

Archie's face had a satisfied glow about it. But something wasn't right.

"Archie," Sam giggled. "Where are your legs?"

The phantom footballer glanced down at his bottom half. His eyes widened as he discovered it wasn't there.

"Mmm," he mused, his bushy eyebrows twitching curiously. "It appears that I am a Legg without legs. And Archibald Legg without legs is like bacon without eggs. Hold on one moment." Archie narrowed his eyes, gazing fixedly at the TV and video to draw electricity into his ghostly figure. Electricity, he'd discovered, gave him strength and energy. He screwed up his face so tightly that his eyebrows and moustache almost met in one great red hairy embrace.

Suddenly, the room seemed to crackle with

electricity. Archie's hair stood up on end as if he'd just had an electric shock. He looked as if he was on fire. Sam and Dan shielded their eyes, dazzled.

After a few moments, the fieriness faded and Archie became clear once more. And now, the children noted, he was complete. Archie registered this fact as well.

"Ah, that's better," he said happily. "Just a small energy problem, nothing to worry about." He sighed contentedly. "Now, how can I assist you?" he asked.

"We wanted to show you these," Dan said. He held out the old shin-pads for Archie to see. Archie's face lit up at once.

"Shin-guards!" he exclaimed. "Excellent, excellent." He took the shin-pads in his hands and gazed at them lovingly. "See how beautifully made they are – just like my own." He glanced down at the large bulge beneath each of his socks.

"They're made of leather, aren't they?" Dan said.

"Indeed they are," Archie enthused. "Very fine leather at that – and lined with wool. You wouldn't suffer sore shins with these on."

"I couldn't play in those," Sam sniffed, tossing back her head. "They're much too heavy. I wouldn't be able to move fast enough."

"Ah, you'd be surprised," said Archie. "Cliff Bastin managed well enough. A faster winger you're never likely to see." The phantom footballer's face took on the warm, respectful expression that it always had when he talked about the Arsenal team of the 1930s or its manager, the great Herbert Chapman. "But, of course," he continued, "it's not how fast you run that's really important. It's how fast you think." He drew himself up proudly. "And, though I say it myself," he added with a twitch of his moustache, "no one thought faster than me."

The two children raised their eyes and sighed.

"The game wasn't as fast in your day, though, was it?" said Dan. "That's what the experts say."

"Oh, do they?" Archie bristled. "Do they indeed? Well I'll tell you, it was a lot harder. If you didn't wear shin-guards, you wouldn't last a day."

"Things are different now," Sam insisted.

"Indeed they are," Archie agreed. "More's the pity. In my day . . ."

His lecture was cut short by an excited exclamation from Dan. "Do you know what, Archie?" he cried. "You should come with us and watch Muddington Rovers play! Then you'd see what football today is really like." His round face beamed with enthusiasm.

Archie looked pleased too. "What an excellent idea," he said. "I should like to see my old team in action again." He nodded contentedly. "I'm sure I could teach them a thing or two . . ."

Chapter Three

ARCHIE SEES RED

Archie was amazed by how much things had changed at Muddington Rovers since his day. For a start, there was the programme. In his time, he said, it had just been a couple of sheets of paper, printed in black and white, costing one penny. His eyes nearly popped out of his head when he saw the present-day, full-colour item – and heard the price.

"£2! For a programme!" he exclaimed. "Why, that's daylight robbery!"

"It is a lot, I agree with you," said Stephen Legg. "Mind you, it's even worse in the Premier League." Muddington Rovers were currently in the second division, having been relegated the season before. When Archie had been a player, the club had been in the top division.

The ground had changed a lot too. The old terraces, on which the crowds had stood to watch matches, had been replaced by seating. There were stands now on all four sides of the pitch. Archie didn't approve. He glared at the rows of seats, many of which were empty, with bristling disdain.

"It may be more comfortable," he sniffed, "but where's the atmosphere? When I played here, the ground was full to the rafters every game. You could hear the tension and excitement in the crowd as you ran on to the pitch."

"Well, the crowd isn't very big today," Dan admitted. "But you'll still hear a roar when the teams come out." He cast a sly glance at Sam, who was sitting the other side of the phantom footballer. "Sam will shriek her head off when she sees Tommy Banks," he said teasingly. "She always does."

Sam's cheeks went as red as her hair. She glowered at her brother. "Of course I cheer when I see him," she said defensively. "He's a great player."

Just moments later, Muddington Rovers arrived on the pitch in their black and green striped shirts. The five children who'd come with Stephen Legg and Archie to the match – Sam, Dan, their cousin Zak, and the twins, Giles and Justin – leapt up excitedly, shouting and clapping with the rest of the crowd. Archie, meanwhile, looked on with quiet interest.

Sam pointed to a shortish, chunky player with spiky blond hair and a small goatee beard. "That's Tommy Banks," she told Archie.

Her ghostly ancestor looked unimpressed. "He seems a bit tubby for a footballer," he remarked with a critical wrinkle of his walrus moustache.

"Wait till you see him play," Sam enthused. "He's the best." She gazed ardently at her footballing hero.

"Yeah, Tommy Banks is cool," said Zak, nodding his head in a waft of black ringlets.

"He's OK," said Dan casually. He glanced at Sam again out of the corner of his eye and she stuck her tongue out at him.

"Now, now," said Archie soothingly. "We're all on the same side."

The game kicked off and Muddington Rovers quickly went on the attack. For the first five minutes, Easthampton, Muddington's opponents, hardly touched the ball. The play was all in the Easthampton half. Tommy Banks was brilliant. He made one chance for his fellow striker, Dean Jones, then had a great shot himself that was saved spectacularly by the keeper.

"See," said Sam, turning to Archie, "I told you he was good, didn't I?"

"Mmm," Archie murmured appreciatively. "He reminds me a little of Alex James, the great Arsenal playmaker."

Sam grinned; this, from Archie, was praise indeed.

Muddington Rovers continued to dominate the game. They had all the play, but just couldn't score the goal they deserved. Dean Jones missed another good chance and Tommy Banks hit the post with a curling free kick from the edge of the penalty area. The crowd groaned with disappointment.

But at last the goal came and, to Sam's particular delight, it was Tommy Banks who scored. He played a clever one-two with Dean Jones, burst past a defender and slotted the ball calmly into the corner of the net.

Once more the crowd stood and cheered. Stephen Legg waved his programme in the air like a flag. Sam, Dan and Zak hugged one another. Giles and Justin smacked hands in a high five. Even Archie was excited. He raised his hands in the air and glowed brightly surrounded by a fiery aura.

At half-time the score was still 1–0.

"Well, Archie, how are the team shaping up, do you think?" Stephen Legg inquired amiably.

Archie stroked his moustache thoughtfully. "They are doing quite well," he said. "But they should have scored more goals." He pursed his lips in a gesture of dissatisfaction. "They need more than two attackers, I should say." Archie favoured the WM formation – a system of playing made popular by Herbert Chapman – with three, sometimes four strikers.

"At least they're winning," said Dan, who was relieved that the Muddington defence hadn't let in any goals for once.

However, this state of affairs didn't last long. Two minutes into the second half, Easthampton equalized with just about their first real attack of the match. A long clearance found the lone Easthampton striker unmarked with only the goalkeeper to beat, which he did quite easily – *too* easily, in fact, according to Archie.

"I could have saved that with my eyes closed," he seethed. No one contradicted him. The children all knew what a good goalkeeper he was. At the end of most Leggs United training sessions he went in goal and no one could score against him.

"I think he did have his eyes closed – that was the problem," Stephen Legg remarked drily.

After Easthampton's early goal, the match became much more evenly balanced. It was also far more competitive than in the first half, with lots of hard tackles, many of which the referee penalized as fouls – greatly to Archie's disgust.

"What's the matter with this referee?" he complained after the whistle had gone for yet another foul. "There was nothing wrong with that challenge."

"You're not allowed to tackle from behind," Dan said.

"But the defender got the ball," Archie protested.

"It doesn't matter," said Zak, who was the family expert on football rules and facts. "If you tackle from behind and you bring down your opponent, it's a foul."

"What poppycock!" exclaimed Archie, outraged. "In my day that would have been applauded as an excellent tackle."

Archie was even more upset when, a moment later, the referee booked the defender who'd made the "foul" tackle. He booked six more during the second half – all quite unfairly, in Archie's opinion. Each time the referee reached for his yellow card, Archie threw up his hands and groaned in dismay. "Defenders wouldn't have lasted two minutes in my day with this lily-livered, whistle-happy ref," he moaned.

It was the final booking of the game that stirred up Archie's fiercest indignation. It came very near the end of the match. Muddington Rovers were attacking, making a final push for the winning goal. A high cross was sent over from the wing, right into the goalmouth. The Easthampton goalkeeper leapt to catch the ball and, as he did so, Dean Jones barged into him, knocking ball and goalie into the net. Archie was on his feet at once, arms raised in jubilation.

"Goal!" he cried and he danced a little jig to celebrate. Then he turned to the others with a huge, hairy grin. "We've won," he declared.

The children laughed. The twins laughed so much they fell off their seats.

"That wasn't a goal, Archie," said Dan.

"He fouled the goalie," said Sam.

"Barging the goalie is against the rules," Zak confirmed.

Archie stared at them for an instant in disbelief. Then he turned back to the pitch and saw that the referee had indeed blown his whistle, not for a goal, but for a free-kick. Not only that, but he was writing Dean Jones' name in his notebook.

Archie saw red. In a flash he whooshed down the aisle between the rows of seats to the edge of the pitch, shaking his fists at the referee and shouting.

"Numbskull! Half-wit! Blind, bald-headed coot!" he screamed.

Archie's outburst, however, was in vain. As the Legg family had already discovered, only they could see and hear Archie; to everyone else he was quite invisible and inaudible. At this particular moment, that was probably a very good thing, Dan thought, as he watched his ghostly ancestor ranting and raving like a madman, his outline ablaze with anger. No, the world definitely wasn't ready for Archie, Dan decided. He was best kept in the family.

Chapter Four

TACKLING PRACTICE

Archie was intrigued but not hugely impressed by his first glimpse of modern-day professional football. The game was faster, he admitted, but he didn't think it was as skilful as in his day. It wasn't nearly as tough either. When he was playing, he said, it was perfectly legal to shoulder-charge the goalkeeper. He'd seen many goals scored that way.

"Football's supposed to be a physical game," Archie stated. Then he told his relatives about a 1934 match between England and Italy, known as the "Battle of Highbury". Seven Arsenal players were in the England team, including the centre forward, Ted Drake. The battle started when he broke the toe of an Italian defender in a tackle. The Italians went mad and retaliated by trying to kick England off the pitch. By the end of the game, nearly all the England players were injured: one had a broken nose, another a broken arm, another an injured ankle, another a cut leg . . .

"But they won," Archie said proudly. "It was a great victory. They didn't hide behind the referee's whistle – they got on with the game like men."

"It sounds more like war than football," Dan remarked.

"Yeah," said Sam. "Girls don't foul like that. We play properly."

"So do boys," said Zak.

"Yes," Dan agreed. "And we tackle too – which is more than you do, Sam."

Before Sam could retort, Archie raised his hand in the air. "As I said before," he boomed, "we're all on the same side here. Save your battling for the opposition on the pitch."

Unlike the older children, the twins thought Archie's story was brilliant. When they got home, they acted out their own Battle of Highbury in the hall. They made such a row that, after a while, Ann Legg appeared with a red card and ordered them both off to bed.

At the next Leggs United training session, Archie concentrated on defensive skills – especially tackling.

"Oh, not tackling," Sam groaned. Everyone knew that Sam thought tackling was boring.

Archie gave her a stern glare. "Tackling is of vital importance," he declared. "If you do not have the ball, you cannot play." He wrinkled his big moustache. "That is a lesson Muddington Rovers would do well to learn," he said. "In particular, that chubby fellow you are so fond of – Piggy Banks, wasn't it?"

"Piggy Banks! Piggy Banks!" repeated the twins and everyone laughed – except Sam. She pushed back her fringe and scowled at Archie.

"His name's *Tommy* Banks," she said fiercely, "and he's not chubby."

"Mmm, well," Archie murmured. "He could do with improving his tackling anyway."

For the tackling practice, Archie paired

everyone up. One player was an attacker and one a defender. The defender had to get the ball off the attacker. Then they swapped round. Sam was partnered with Dan. He was the best tackler in the team and he got the ball off Sam quite easily. But she couldn't get the ball off him – not that she tried very hard.

"You're too big," she complained bitterly. Dan was a good head taller than his sister and he was a lot broader.

"The bigger they are, the harder they fall," Archie commented, hands on hips. "Tackling is as much about timing as strength. Make your tackle at the right moment and you take the ball; time your tackle wrongly and you get nothing – except perhaps a bruise . . . or a booking." He frowned disapprovingly, remembering the Muddington Rovers match. "Allow me to demonstrate."

Archie got Sam to run at him with the ball three times. The first time he lunged at the ball before Sam had reached him and she easily sidestepped the tackle. The second time, Archie waited until Sam was almost past him before trying to tackle, and once again

Sam evaded him easily. The rest of the team cheered.

"Go for it, Sam!" Zak called. Sam wrinkled her small, freckly nose and grinned triumphantly. Then she prepared to take on Archie for a third time.

She rolled the ball in front of her, keeping it close to her feet, confident that she could beat her ghostly ancestor. She moved closer, swaying, waiting for the challenge . . . and whoomf! Suddenly, the ball was no longer there. She looked down in astonishment then turned to see Archie behind her with the ball at

his feet. It had all happened so fast and she hadn't felt a thing.

"Wow!" she said in deep admiration. "That was so quick."

"Cool!" Zak enthused.

"What a tackle! How did you do that?" Dan asked, equally amazed.

Archie waggled his moustache and glowed. "Practice, just practice," he said with a shrug. Then he raised one eyebrow. "Oh, and genius, of course," he added smugly.

Chapter Five

AN UNWELCOME VISITOR

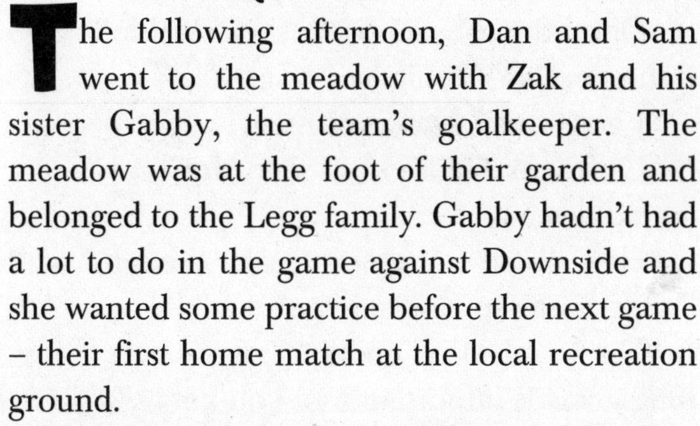

The following afternoon, Dan and Sam went to the meadow with Zak and his sister Gabby, the team's goalkeeper. The meadow was at the foot of their garden and belonged to the Legg family. Gabby hadn't had a lot to do in the game against Downside and she wanted some practice before the next game – their first home match at the local recreation ground.

"I need some proper practice too," Sam declared, "after all that *tackling* yesterday." She darted a sharp glance at Dan. "Let's do some shooting," she said.

"We could have a competition," Zak suggested.

"Yes, good idea," Sam agreed quickly. She and Zak both looked at Dan.

"Suits me," Dan said nonchalantly.

For the next half hour or so, Sam, Dan and Zak took it in turns to fire shots at Gabby, keeping count of the goals they managed to score. Zak and Sam tied with eight goals each; Dan only had three.

"I'm a defender, not a striker," Dan reminded them.

"Good thing," said Sam. "You couldn't score if the goal was as big as a house."

"I got three," Dan protested.

"Only cos Gabby felt sorry for you," Sam jeered.

"He's good at *stopping* goals, though," said Zak, coming to Dan's defence.

"Yes," said Dan, nodding vigorously. "Stopping goals is important too, you know."

Sam tossed her head dismissively. "Huh," she humphed. Stopping goals, like tackling, was something she had no interest in.

Gabby had to go off to her gymnastics club,

so the other three children practised passing for a while. Then they sat down at the edge of the pitch to rest.

"Who are we playing next in the league?" asked Sam.

"Weldon Wanderers," said Zak.

Dan nodded. "I bet they'll be a lot tougher than Downside," he said.

"They couldn't be worse," Sam remarked.

"No, not unless they all had one leg," Dan laughed.

He looked up and the smile quickly vanished from his face, as he spotted a familiar, unwelcome figure peering at him over the fence. It was his arch-rival, Perry Nolan.

"What are you doing here?" Dan demanded coolly.

Perry pulled a face. "Just looking," he said. "No crime in that, is there?"

"Well, now you've looked, you can clear off," said Dan shortly.

Perry scowled. "You can't tell me what to do," he said. "I'm not one of your stupid team."

"We wouldn't have you," Sam said sharply. "We don't like cheats."

"No," said Dan. Earlier in the summer, when Leggs United had played Perry Nolan's team, Muddington Colts, in the Holt Nolan Football Challenge, Perry had dived outrageously to get a penalty. His dad, Holt Nolan, had been the referee. "You're just jealous cos we beat you," Dan jibed.

"You were lucky," said Perry. "Wait till we play you in the league."

"We'll just beat you again," said Dan defiantly.

"Yeah, wait till you come down to the rec," Sam added fierily. "You won't stand a chance."

Perry sneered. "Yeah?" he scoffed. "We thrashed Ledminster 8–0 last week. I got a hat-trick." Perry was always boasting about how good he was and how many goals he'd scored. It was one of the reasons why Dan disliked him so much.

"They must have been really useless," he sniped. "Or was your dad the ref again?"

"We beat Downside away," Zak said matter-of-factly.

"And on Saturday we're going to beat Weldon Wanderers," Sam added confidently.

This news had a dramatic effect on Perry. "Weldon Wanderers!" he exclaimed. "You're playing Weldon Wanderers on Saturday?"

"Yeah. What of it?" said Dan.

Perry's face broke into a huge gloating smile. "You'll see," he said, and he laughed. "You'd better get that lucky ball of yours – cos you're going to need it." He tapped his bike helmet. "You should get yourselves some of these too," he added. Then, still sniggering, he rode away on his bike, tooting his horn as he went.

"What do you think he meant?" Zak asked,

his large brown eyes looking unusually troubled.

"Oh, nothing," shrugged Dan. "He's just trying to wind us up, that's all. Ignore him."

"Yeah," said Sam swaggeringly. "We're not scared of anyone." Her face creased in a freckly grin. "We've got Archie, haven't we?"

Chapter Six

ARCHIE SHOWS HOW

Over the next day or so, Perry Nolan's comments about Weldon Wanderers kept nagging at Dan. What had he meant exactly? *Why* would Leggs United need luck? *Why* would they need crash helmets? It was all rubbish probably, as he'd said at the time, but, well, what if there *was* something in what Perry had said? He should at least mention it to Archie, he decided.

At the next training session, Dan took Archie to one side. He spoke casually, as if he didn't really believe there was anything in Perry's talk – and he was quite relieved that Archie seemed to think the same.

"Sounds like a lot of poppycock," Archie scoffed with a flourish of his walrus moustache. "Besides, it's Leggs United that concerns me, laddy, not Weldon Wanderers." He eyed his captain with a steely gaze. "When I've finished with you," he intoned gravely, "you'll be more than a match for any team. Mark my words."

Archie was a good coach. He said it often enough himself – and, though they groaned when he did, his team agreed. Every one of them benefited from his skills training and tactical guidance.

He gave Gabby lots of shot practice – low shots into the corners especially, making her dive from side to side to improve her stretch. Herbert Chapman had done something similar with his goalkeeper, he explained.

As well as tackling techniques, he taught Dan and the twins about marking and covering. And he practised heading with Zak's brother, Rollo, who was the oldest and tallest player in the team.

"We need a target man at corners and free-kicks," Archie told him. "You could be our Ted Drake."

"But don't start any battles," joked Dan, who was standing nearby with Zak and Sam. Then the three of them laughed, because Rollo was the least aggressive person they knew. They'd never heard him raise his voice in anger, never mind get in a fight.

"Never mind the Battle of Highbury," sniffed Archie in disgust. "You're not even allowed to tackle properly these days."

The phantom coach set Sam and Zak a passing test, with two of the triplets, Ben and Frances, as their partners. They were both very fast runners and played on the wings.

In Archie's exercise, Ben had to kick the ball to Sam and then sprint forwards to get the return pass. Frances did the same with Zak. The real test for Sam and Zak was that they had to kick their passes over the top of a tall board that Archie had set up, and make the ball land just in front of the sprinting winger. If the pass was too far ahead or behind, or to one side, it was considered a failure.

To begin with, Sam and Zak failed a lot.

"This is too hard," Sam complained after ten minutes or so. "I'll never get it right."

"Rome wasn't built in a day," Archie remarked primly. "Practice makes perfect."

"You show us, then," Sam challenged her coach.

Archie wiggled his caterpillar eyebrows. "Very well," he said. He got Ben to kick the ball to him, then, glancing up, he placed the ball perfectly in the path of the speeding winger. Then he did the same thing on the other side with Frances. He turned to the cousins with a satisfied smile. All around his figure a hazy aura glowed.

"Cool!" said Zak admiringly.

"All right, you win," said Sam. Then she and Zak continued their practice – with increasing success.

With Zoe and Jack (the oldest of the triplets by two minutes), Archie worked mainly on balance and ball control. They were both reasonable players but were sometimes a little clumsy. In order to correct this, Archie marked out a line of large flowerpots and got the two children to weave in and out, keeping the ball close to their feet.

After a while, he moved the flowerpots closer together, then closer still . . . Then he set up a wooden plank above the ground, resting on the pots. Zoe and Jack had to move backwards and forwards across it, going faster each time.

Now and then, not surprisingly, one or the other fell off – but there wasn't far to fall. Once, Zoe lost her balance and dropped right on to Archie. Her glasses flew off and landed in his hair. Archie caught his young relative and lifted her high into the air for an instant, before placing her back on the plank again.

At that moment the postman happened to be passing the meadow. Glancing over the fence, he was astonished to see a girl and a pair of glasses floating in the air! It gave him such a shock that he crashed his bike into the fence. His mailbag fell off and letters scattered everywhere.

The children quickly ran to help him. Archie lent a hand too, picking up letters and returning them to the sack. But this only caused the poor postman more confusion – it looked to him as

if the letters were flying through the air by themselves! He blinked hard and shook his head.

"I'm not myself today, kids," he said with a dazed expression. Then, woozily, he got back on his bike and wobbled away up the road.

"He looks like he's seen a ghost," laughed Dan.

"Mmm," Archie murmured critically. "In my day, of course, postmen were made of much stronger stuff . . ."

Chapter Seven

PITCHING IN

At breakfast on Wednesday morning Stephen Legg had some bad news.

"Our pitch at the rec has fallen through," he told Sam and Dan gloomily. "It seems they double booked it by mistake. Another team had already reserved it."

"But can't we just play on one of the other pitches?" Dan asked.

Stephen Legg shook his head. "They're all booked," he said. "There are a few other places I could try, but I don't hold out much hope. It's very late now."

Dan tugged at his ear thoughtfully. "So what

happens if we can't get another pitch? Will we have to postpone the match?"

Stephen Legg sighed and ran his fingers through his beard. "I'm afraid not, Dan," he said sadly. "If we don't have a pitch by Saturday, then we have to concede the game to Weldon Wanderers."

"But that's not fair," Sam complained. "They win without having to play."

"It's in the league rules," Stephen Legg said mournfully.

Throughout the day, with increasing desperation, Stephen and Ann Legg phoned up parks and sports grounds in the area to try and find a new home ground for Leggs United. But by the end of the afternoon they had had no success. Everywhere was booked.

It was a very long-faced Sam who summoned Archie from the ball that evening. Next to her, Dan and Zak were looking equally miserable.

Oddly, however, their ghostly ancestor was not downcast at the children's news.

"Well, these things happen," he said calmly, with a twitch of his moustache. "It's of little matter."

The three children stared at him as if he were mad.

"Don't you understand, Archie?" Sam exclaimed. "If we don't have a pitch, then we can't play in the league."

Archie looked at Sam pitifully. "But we do have a pitch, laddy," he said. "Well, we have a ground, in any case."

"Where? What ground?" Dan quizzed his phantom relative.

Archie beamed. "Why, here, of course," he said. "The meadow."

"The meadow!" cried Sam.

"Cool," said Zak.

"But it's got no lines or goalposts or anything," Dan protested.

Archie waved a pale hand dismissively. "That's easily settled, laddy," he said lightly. "It just needs a bit of hard toil and teamwork."

"My dad'll help!" Zak cried with uncharacteristic excitement. "I'll go and ask him now . . ."

Archie's suggestion was met with universal approval by his relatives. It was the obvious solution. The worry was whether the job could be completed in time. There were just two days to go before the Weldon match and there was lots to be done. Everyone would have to lend a hand – adults and children alike. Fortunately, the children were still on their summer holiday.

"It'll be great fun," Dan enthused. He couldn't wait to get started.

"Well, it'll be better than tackling practice, anyway," said Sam.

So it was agreed: the three families would spend the next couple of days trying to turn the meadow into a proper football pitch.

Next morning, the work began. Zak's father, Otis Browne, was a carpenter and he worked on building the goal frames. Ann Legg and Nadya Legg (the triplets' mother) were responsible for making the goal nets. Julia Browne's task was to make sure that the pitch was properly marked out and that the lines were all in their correct place. She borrowed a line-marker from Muddington Primary School where she was a teacher. Mark Legg supplied a motorized lawnmower from his garage, Legg's Motors, to cut the grass.

Stephen Legg was the only one of the parents

who didn't have a definite job. He wandered around, making lots of suggestions – most of which were quite impractical. Eventually, Ann Legg sent him off to inform the relevant people about Leggs United's change of ground.

"We don't want to do all this work and have no one turn up because they don't know where to come," she said.

"Very true," Stephen Legg agreed. "I'll go and phone the league secretary straight away."

The children all did their bit, too. Zak and Rollo helped their dad with building the goalposts and bar – and then painting them. Their little brother Max Browne, who was five, joined in as well. But he mainly painted himself. By the time the frame was finished, he was streaked all over in white paint.

"I think he's trying to look ghostly like his great-great-uncle Archie," laughed Otis Browne, shaking his head at the state of his youngest child.

"He looks more like a badger," said Zak.

"Or a skunk," suggested Rollo.

"Yeah – I'm a smelly skunk," said Max and,

going down on all fours, he chased his little cousin Flora across the meadow.

The job the children liked best was cutting the grass. They took it in turns to sit up next to Mark or Stephen Legg on the motor mower and trundle noisily across the meadow, churning up grass in their wake. Mark Legg let some of the older children – Dan, Sam and Zoe – have a go at driving the mower themselves. He showed them how to steer the mower so that it cut a straight strip of grass and then how to stop and turn the machine and how to change gear. There was only one nasty moment, when Sam took her hands off the steering wheel for a moment to wave to her mum and the mower veered to the left, bashing into the fence.

"Oh, well," shrugged Otis Browne, looking at the splintered fencing. "I needed to put a gate in the fence somewhere. I guess I'll just put it there."

Dan loved the mower – and so did Archie. He said it reminded him of the motor cars of his youth. Once, when Dan was driving, Archie rode along too. He stood at the back of the mower, radiant with pleasure, head held high – "like a king, surveying his kingdom", Stephen Legg said. And Dan reckoned that was right, because Archie's kingdom *was* the football pitch. That was where he reigned supreme. Not that Dan would tell his ghostly relative that – he was big-headed enough already!

The trickiest task was getting all the pitch measurements right and marking out the lines. Julia Browne's patience was sorely tested – particularly by the twins, Giles and Justin. They were supposed to be helping her by acting as

markers, but they kept getting distracted and running off to look at other things.

"Give me strength!" she exclaimed several times, as she looked up to see the other end of the tape measure wandering away over the meadow. Still, with the new school year less than a week away, trying to organize the twins was good preparation for what was to come, she said. Teaching her new class would be easy in comparison.

By Friday morning, the grass was all cut, but there was still a lot left to do.

"We'll never be ready," said Sam wearily, as she looked at the half of the pitch that still needed to be marked up.

"Yes, we will," Dan replied stirringly. "We've got to be." He ran over to help Julia with the line painting and, after a short rest, Sam joined him. They took over from the twins and immediately things started to move along faster.

By late Friday afternoon, the pitch was finished. All that remained was for the goals to be put up. Everyone was exhausted, but happy.

"We've done it," said Dan, looking with pride at the transformed meadow. "We've got a pitch."

"It looks great!" Sam confirmed, smiling broadly for the first time in two days. "Like a real football ground."

All the hard work, everyone agreed, had been worthwhile.

Archie was a little more critical. He gave the pitch a thorough inspection, pointing out a couple of places where the lines were a little bit blobby or not entirely straight. He found a few bumps too. But all in all, he appeared to be satisfied.

"Well, it's not exactly Highbury, but it will do," was his verdict. Then his serious expression relaxed into a glowing smile. “I believe Herbert Chapman would approve,” he remarked contentedly.

Chapter Eight

BUTTERFLIES

Saturday was a fine day. The sun shone brightly in a blue, cloudless sky. Straight after breakfast Dan and Sam went to look at their new pitch. They passed the twins, Giles and Justin, who were racing snails on the lawn. It was hard to know which of the snails was winning, though, because they were going in opposite directions.

"You two," said Sam and she tapped her head to show that she thought they were completely mad. Then she followed Dan down to the meadow.

The goals were up now, with their nets. They gleamed white in the dewy sunshine. Dan and

Sam stood by the wall, taking in the scene before them and marvelling at how fresh and new it all looked.

"I'm glad we're playing here, rather than at the rec," Dan said dreamily. "It seems more special somehow." He tugged on his ear thoughtfully. "This really is *our* ground," he added proudly.

"Yes," said Sam. "And we're going to start with a win." She ran forward and banged a ball into one of the goals.

The morning really dragged, but at last lunchtime came, and after that, the countdown to the match at two o'clock. In that final hour before kick-off, Dan's stomach was filled with butterflies; he just couldn't wait for the game to start.

Archie had instructed Dan to gather the team together at quarter to two. As they assembled, Sam summoned the phantom manager from the old ball. He blazed out as if fired from a cannon.

"Right," he said, shimmering with energy, "I believe it is time for my team talk." He cast an approving eye over his players, crowded into the large sitting room of number 15 Poplar Street. They were all dressed in their smart team strip, which had been provided by Mark Legg. "I see we are ready to motor," he remarked playfully, nodding at the words *Legg's Motors* on the front of the team's shirts.

He coughed and his face took on a serious expression. "Now," he said gravely, his hairy eyebrows coming together in an upside down V, "this afternoon's game will be an historic occasion: the first ever competitive football match to be played at The Meadow, the new home ground of Leggs United." He paused momentarily before continuing: "To we Leggs – and Brownes – this is an event as momentous as the first ever Cup Final played at Wembley in 1923. Bolton beat West Ham by two goals to nil that day and one of the scorers was David Jack, who, as you know, was later signed by Herbert Chapman to play for Arsenal in that great forward line." Archie paused once more, shimmering with emotion, his eyes full of the awe they always held when he mentioned the great manager or his team. "This afternoon," he went on, his voice quivering with feeling, "I want you to play for me, as Arsenal played for Herbert Chapman."

Archie's words were met, at first, by total silence. His team were taken aback by the serious tone of his speech and not really sure how to react. Some of the younger members were quite bemused. It was Dan who finally found his tongue.

"Does that mean you want us to win?" he asked hesitantly.

Archie frowned. "Win?" he repeated, his whole body glowing. "Why, of course I want you to win, laddy. But winning's just part of the story. I want you to display the full range of skills and tactical brilliance that I, Archibald Legg, have taught you." He pursed his lips disapprovingly. "I would ask for some of the fighting spirit too," he sniffed, "but of course that is not part of the game nowadays, more is the pity."

"We may not fight, but we've got plenty of spirit," Sam protested. She turned to face the rest of the team. "Haven't we, Leggs United?"

"Yes!" came the loud and unanimous reply.

This response seemed to satisfy Archie. "Good, good," he said happily. Then, in one amazingly fluid movement, the phantom footballer dragged back the old ball with one foot, flicked it into the air and caught it on the end of his finger, where it span like a top. "Now, follow me to the pitch," he commanded. "I have something to show you."

Archie led his team down the garden, over the wall, and into the meadow. There they discovered Otis Browne, painting something behind one of the goals, with the line-marking whitewash. As Archie and the children approached, Otis gave a final dab with his brush and stood up straight. Dan, who was right behind Archie, was the first to see a kind of diagram, with a lot of lines and initials.

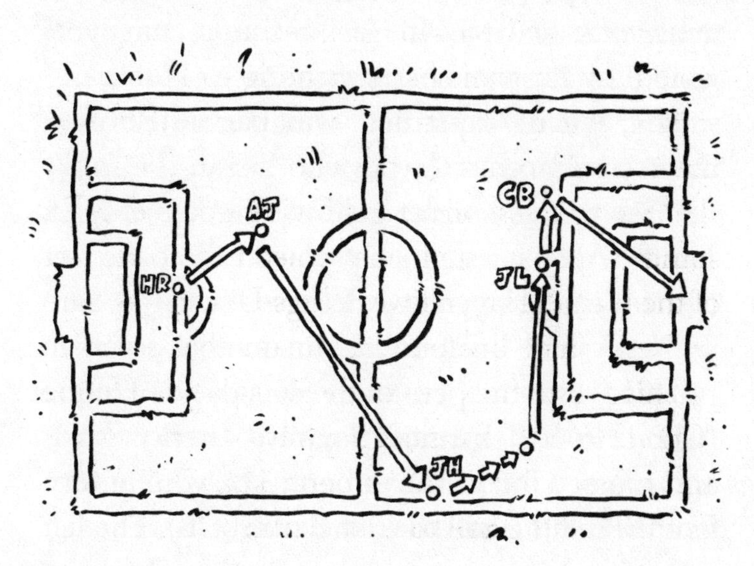

"There, all done," Otis murmured. He turned to Archie. "Is that how you wanted it, coach?" he enquired.

Archie put his hands on his hips and nodded. His face was rosy with contentment. "Excellent," he enthused. "Quite excellent."

"What is it?" asked Dan, who was standing right next to his ghostly relative now. The rest of the team were clustered around the curious painted diagram, studying it with a collective air of puzzlement.

"That," said Archie, wiggling his moustache theatrically, "is a picture of the most perfect goal ever scored. In ten seconds, this goal scored by Arsenal changed the face of football."

HR, Archie explained, was Herbie Roberts, the Arsenal centre back, who began the move that led to the wonder goal with a pass to Alex James (AJ). James quickly played the ball over the top of the opposing defence (much as Sam and Zak had been trying to do that week in practice) into the path of the speedy Joe Hulme (JH). He had sprinted forward twenty yards and crossed for Jack Lambert (JL), who in turn had flicked the ball to Cliff Bastin (CB). The left winger had wasted no time in banging the ball into the net.

"Nothing could be more perfect," Archie declared ecstatically, "and that is why I asked Otis to draw it here, right next to the pitch, where it will serve, I hope, as an inspiration to you all every time you set foot on this field." He looked around at his rather puzzled team with a serene expression.

As he was doing so, a tall figure dressed in black appeared at the meadow gate. "Looks like your ref's arrived. Someone had better go and open the gate," said Otis Browne sensibly.

At that moment, a packed mini-van drew into the road behind the meadow.

"Here's our opposition, too," Dan said and he had that butterflies-in-the-stomach feeling again – only now it felt as if the butterflies were all fluttering wildly. It was time, finally, for the game to begin.

Chapter Nine

NO PRISONERS

From the moment they marched into The Meadow, Dan had a bad feeling about Weldon Wanderers. For a start, they were all so big – bigger than most of the Leggs players. Only Dan, Zoe and Rollo matched up to them. They looked tough too – most of them had close-cropped hair and hard, staring eyes.

When the referee called the two captains for the toss-up, the Weldon Wanderers skipper spat on the grass and strolled to the centre circle. He had very short hair and a gold stud in one ear.

"My name's Paul Starkey," said the ref, offering his hand to Dan. He was a very big man with a smiley face that Dan found reassuring. He looked like a ref who'd be fair and keep good control of the game.

"I'm Dan Legg," Dan replied, shaking the ref's hand.

The ref nodded and turned to the other captain.

"Ricky," growled the Weldon Wanderers leader, barely touching the ref's outstretched hand. His face bore a hostile scowl.

"OK, Ricky, Dan," the ref said amicably, taking a coin from his pocket. "Who's going to call?"

"He can," Ricky muttered with a stiff nod at Dan.

The referee flipped the coin.

"Heads," called Dan.

"Heads it is," said the ref.

"We'll kick off," said Dan. "Which end would you like?" he asked his opposing captain.

"It don't matter," said Ricky. He glanced at the pitch about him as if it were a rubbish dump. "We'll stay where we are," he ventured at last. Then he turned and jogged back to his team.

As Leggs United lined up for the kick-off in their WM formation, Dan was glad he was wearing shin-pads. Somehow he reckoned he was going to need them in this game. Sam wasn't wearing any as usual. Well, that was her lookout. She probably wouldn't get into any tackles anyway, Dan thought, knowing what she was like.

On the touchline, the three sets of parents were together in a group by Archie, who was in his usual match stance – standing near the centre line with one foot on the old ball and his hands on his hips. There was a shimmering aura about him. He looked cool and collected. But, Dan wondered, for how long?

Dan clapped his hands. "Right, Leggs, let's go!" he exhorted. But his call was drowned by a much louder, deeper, harsher shout from the touchline.

"Right, no prisoners, Weldon! Let's get stuck in!"

Looking over in the direction of the cry, Dan saw a burly, bald-headed man in a blue shell-suit. He was standing just a few metres from Archie, who was staring at him now with a slightly baffled air. His attention was quickly diverted back to the pitch, though, when the ref blew his whistle for the game to begin.

It took Weldon Wanderers about five seconds to make their mark. No sooner had Zak kicked the ball to Sam, than Ricky was on to her. She took the ball, looked up to make a pass and *wham!* The Weldon skipper clattered into her with a tackle that left her hopping with pain. But it was a fair tackle, he won the ball

cleanly, and straight away the visitors were on the attack.

Dan was busier in the opening ten minutes of this match than he'd been in the entire game against Downside. Time after time he was called upon to make crucial tackles and interceptions as Weldon Wanderers pressed forward. But after every clearance he made, the ball just came straight back. The visitors were as tough as they looked – they tackled like tigers and harried any Leggs player who had the ball.

Poor Sam couldn't get a kick – well, not of the ball anyway. She got plenty of kicks on her legs. Zak fared no better. Any time the ball came near him he found himself surrounded by big, muscular defenders, who easily shrugged him aside. It was the same story out on the wings with Ben and Frances. With Sam being so tightly marked, they hardly got a chance to run – and when they did it was in vain.

Leggs United were pinned in their own half. Only desperate defending by Dan and the twins, brilliant keeping by Gabby and some very poor shooting by the Weldon forwards prevented the away team from taking a big lead.

As the half went on, the pressure mounted and mounted. Weldon poured forward, winning corner after corner . . .

Finally their pressure told. A third successive corner saw the ball crossed to the far side of the Leggs United six-yard box. Gabby leapt to push the ball away, but the huge Weldon centre half jumped too, towering above her, and nodded the ball into the goal. On the line, Zoe made a brave attempt to stop the ball, but the header was too strong. The ball flew into the net and so did Zoe's glasses. Fortunately, they didn't break.

On the touchline, the Wanderers' coach shook a fist and snarled, "Come on, Weldon! Take them apart now. No prisoners!"

Archie's reaction to these aggressive commands was to give his opposing coach a fizzing stare. "This is a game of football, not a war," he declared indignantly, wagging one bony finger. But, of course, he got no response, for only his own players could see or hear him.

Weldon Wanderers were really fired up now.

The goal and their coach's instructions seemed to make them more competitive than ever. They made full use of their height and weight advantage and their play became even more physical. Some of their challenges drew the displeasure of the referee, but most didn't. When Sam complained about the tackling, the ref just smiled and shook his head.

"Football's a hard game, son," he said airily. Sam glared back at him from under her fringe.

What the referee didn't see were all the nudges, pokes and sly kicks carried out by the Weldon players behind his back. Archie saw, though. He glowered and fumed on the touchline, screaming at the ref to take action. He vented his anger on the Weldon coach and players too.

"Foulers! Dirty cheats! Hooligans!" he cried furiously, as Sam received yet another tap on the shins well away from where the play was.

Finally, Archie could take no more. When Zak was felled by another crunching tackle from the Weldon skipper and the referee waved *Play on*, Archie flared with indignation. But this was nothing compared to his absolute outrage when the move that followed resulted in Weldon Wanderers' second goal – scored by the offending player himself, Ricky.

As the ball hit the back of the Leggs United net, Archie rampaged onto the pitch, glowing as if radioactive. His red hair stood up on end, quivering with electricity.

"Don't you know a foul when you see one!" he shouted angrily at the ref. "Or are you afraid you might wear out your whistle if you blew it?"

At this instant, as if literally adding insult to injury, the referee did indeed blow his whistle. He gave it three loud blasts.

"Half-time!" he announced. Then he trotted away to the side of the pitch, leaving Archie smouldering in his wake.

Chapter Ten

A MINOR RESHUFFLE

At half-time, the Leggs United players sat on the grass and nursed their bruises, while their parents tried to comfort and encourage them. Archie perched on the old ball with his shoulders hunched like a huge sulky eagle.

Julia Browne handed round slices of orange to the team, but she refused to do the same for the visitors – or the referee. Like Archie she was furious about the tackle on Zak that had led to Weldon's second goal.

"It's only a game, Julia," Stephen Legg said, adopting his most soothing doctor's bedside manner.

"Huh," his sister huffed. "That boy could have broken Zak's leg."

Archie nodded vigorously in agreement. "Indeed, he could have," he said. "It was a disgraceful tackle. In my day, it would never have been allowed."

"I thought in your day the game was much tougher," Dan reminded his manager.

"Yes, well, it was," Archie blustered. "Tougher – but fair."

"I've a good mind to have a word with that referee," Julia Browne remarked sharply.

"I'm OK, Mum, really," said Zak hastily – but the marks on his legs told a different tale.

"Now I know why Perry was looking so smug," Dan said ruefully. "He knew what the Wanderers were like."

"I wish I had," winced Sam. "Then I'd definitely have got myself some shin-pads. My left leg is aching all over."

"They are a hard team," Archie conceded grudgingly. "But, I believe, there is a soft centre. We just have to uncover it."

"They certainly keep it well hidden," Sam remarked. She sucked on her orange, wondering gloomily what the second half would bring. If it was more of the same, then she'd rather not play at all – not that she'd ever admit that to Archie, of course. She wasn't going to give him the chance to say all that stuff about football being a man's game. She'd had quite enough of that from the ref. It was all very well for him to talk, she thought bitterly; he was huge. If he was a player, no one would dare to clatter into him.

Archie, meanwhile, was on his feet again. He had a brief, whispered chat with Stephen Legg, who turned and hurried away in the direction of his house. Then the phantom coach came and stood among his players.

"Right," he said, fixing the children with a fiery stare. "I believe I have the solution. There is nothing wrong with the formation we are playing. Defensively we have been excellent, despite the two goals. All that is required is a minor reshuffle."

Archie's reshuffle involved Rollo taking Zak's place as the spearhead of the attack. "We need some extra height and weight up front," he explained. Zak was to drop back and play alongside Sam, with Zoe partnering Jack.

"But how can we get the ball up to Rollo?" Sam grumbled. She gestured at the opposing team. "They just don't give us any time."

Archie raised his hand imperiously. His hairy eyebrows hopped like frisky caterpillars. "Now, now, laddy," he said, and before Sam could correct him he continued, "I've thought of that. Am I not Archibald Legg, master strategist, tactical genius, Herbert Chapman's spiritual heir . . ."

The children groaned.

"Just tell us what you're going to do," said Sam.

Archie glared at her. "I want you and Zak to play further back in your own half," he explained, "behind Zoe and Jack and in front of Dan and the twins, Charles and Martin."

"Giles and Justin!" shrieked the twins as one.

"Mmm, just so," Archie murmured fuzzily. "Zoe and Jack will act as a kind of shield, preventing that hoodlum captain from getting to you and Zak too quickly. You must use the extra time you will have to make your passes count." He looked across pointedly at the whitewash diagram of Arsenal's ten-second wonder goal. "I want to see some goals this half – in *their* net, not ours."

"We'll do our best," Dan said. "Won't we, team?"

"Yes," came the reply, but it didn't sound very convincing.

Sam hobbled to her feet. She grimaced and held out her left leg. "If I get any more kicks on this leg, I reckon it's going to be too sore to play with," she said grimly.

She glanced across at Zak, who was gently rubbing his right leg. "Zak's leg is pretty bad too," she added.

To her surprise, Archie actually looked sympathetic. "Help is at hand, laddy," he said with a small smile.

No sooner had Archie spoken than Stephen Legg appeared with a red face.

"I've got them, Archie," he said breathlessly and he handed over to his ghostly ancestor the ancient pair of bulky shin-guards.

"Just the job," said Archie warmly, clutching the leather guards with affection. He offered

one to Zak and one to Sam. "Put those under the socks on your kicking legs," he instructed.

"But they're huge," Sam protested.

"Precisely," said Archie.

Then, as the referee's whistle blew to summon the teams for the second half, he turned towards the opposition with an icy gaze. "Now we'll see who takes no prisoners," he remarked coolly.

Chapter Eleven

RAISED SPIRITS

Archie's half-time talk had immediate results. Breaking up Weldon Wanderers' first attack, Dan fed the ball to Sam in her new deep position. For once, she found herself in space and with time to look up and consider the situation. She took a couple of strides forward and then whipped a long diagonal pass over the Weldon midfield towards the wing, where Frances was already sprinting forward, leaving her marker behind. The ball dropped perfectly between Frances and the Weldon full-back. Now fully in her stride, the youngest Legg triplet reached the ball well before the defender and was on her way past him before he could adjust to get a tackle in.

It was the first real opportunity Frances had had to run at the Weldon defence in the whole match and she wasn't going to waste it. On and on she raced until she reached the byline, where she chipped a perfect cross into the heart of the Weldon penalty area.

The pace and precision of the move caught the Weldon central defenders napping. Neither of them jumped to cut out the cross and nor did the goalie. It was as if they each expected one of the others to deal with the ball – or maybe, considering how little they'd had to do in the first half, they didn't think there was any danger. But if that was the case, they were wrong.

As the cross arrived at the far post, Rollo flung himself forward and met the ball full on the forehead. It may not have been the most elegant of headers, but it was highly effective. The ball rocketed into the top of the net. Leggs United had struck back with their first attack of the second half.

"Goal!" Stephen Legg cried and he hugged

his sister. The other Legg spectators were just as excited.

"Great header, son!" shouted Otis Browne.

"Let's have another now, Leggs!" Mark Legg called.

On the touchline, the Weldon coach was furious. He shouted and swore and shook his fist at his players, angry with them for their slack defending.

"You dozy bunch of clowns!" he yelled.

Archie, by contrast, remained quite still and seemingly aloof from all the noise and passion around him. But his face betrayed his feelings in the shape of a huge satisfied grin. With its speed, directness and simplicity, the goal had been in the style of the Arsenal ten-second wonder goal itself. Archie had pulled off another tactical master stroke and he knew it.

The goal certainly lifted Leggs United. They played with new vigour and spirit. Protected by Zoe and Jack, Sam and Zak saw a lot more of the ball and were able to display their skills. They raked passes to the wings, dribbled past opponents, and had a couple of shots each.

Meanwhile, up front, Rollo's height and strength gave the visitors plenty to think about. He was the tallest player on the field and they couldn't knock him off the ball as they had Zak. The heading practice he'd done proved very useful too – and not only with the goal. Several times during the half he beat the Weldon defenders in the air to set up good attacking positions for other players. From one of these, Sam rattled the crossbar with a scorching drive.

The match was less tough than in the first half, probably because the Weldon team started to tire, but there was still plenty of rough tackling.

Twice in a matter of minutes, Ben was scythed to the ground by his marker as he set off on a flying run down the wing. Both times, the referee blew for a foul, but he took no further action. He just wagged his finger at the offending player and told him not to do it again.

After the second occasion, however, Archie leapt off his ball in a blazing fury. His face went as red as his hair.

"Take his name, send him off!" he screeched at the ref. "Are you afraid to use your pencil as well as your whistle? What's the matter with you, man?" His anger flared up even more when he heard the Weldon coach applauding his defender.

"You scoundrel!" Archie shouted. "You should be ashamed of yourself." He fizzed with frustration at his inability to make himself heard.

Within a couple of minutes, Weldon Wanderers, in the form of Ricky, committed another blatant foul, this time on Frances. A howl of outrage went up from the Leggs United supporters. The referee blew his whistle and awarded Leggs United a free-kick.

"Keep it clean, son," he said mildly, waving the Weldon skipper away. Ricky turned round with a smirk and spat on the grass – and that was when Archie decided enough was enough.

It was time for him to act.

Chapter Twelve
SUPERGHOST!

One moment Archie was on the touchline, the next he was out on the pitch, fully charged and ready for action.

"What are you doing, Archie?" said Dan, as Archie jogged past him.

"I have come to uphold fair play," Archie replied mysteriously, touching one bony finger to his nose.

Dan shook his head and sighed. Next to him, the Weldon central striker was gaping at Dan as if he thought he was mad. Dan made no attempt to explain why he appeared to be talking to thin air. After all, if he told the truth – that he was talking to a ghost – his opponent would think him even crazier! Besides, Dan was much more interested in what Archie was up to.

He didn't have to wait long to find out. The next time Leggs United went on the attack, Zak lofted another ball over the Weldon midfield into the path of Ben. Once again the middle of the Legg triplets was faced by the Weldon defender who had recently fouled him. Once again, he zipped past him. Once again, the defender's foot went out to bring Ben down . . . Only this time he didn't make contact. Archie nipped in between the two players and tripped the defender up. As Ben ran on, the Weldon player fell over on his backside with a very surprised look on his face.

The next to receive Archie's justice was the Weldon skipper himself. As Sam swerved past him, Ricky moved across to block her and barge her off the ball. Instead of bumping into Sam, though, he found himself colliding with an invisible wall that sent him stumbling backwards. As Sam sprinted on, Ricky stood, gaping with incredulity. "What the . . .?" he muttered, scratching his head.

Archie was everywhere. He was a ghostly dynamo, pulsing with energy. He charged all over the field like a phantom superhero, protecting his players from unfair treatment. He repelled elbow blows, got in the way of ankle-taps, shin-kicks, trips and pushes, and generally flung himself about to prevent foul play.

However, there was a downside to Archie's interventions. The Leggs United players were so mesmerized by his antics that they found it hard to keep their minds on the game. Pass after pass went astray and the few scoring chances they had, they failed to take. Rollo was the main culprit. Scoring goals was not his strength and he missed at least three good chances that Zak would surely have taken. As the match drew to a close, it was still 2–1 to Weldon Wanderers.

Leggs United mounted one last attack down the wing and Ben won a corner. Sam raced over to take the kick. Standing in his own half, Dan glanced across at the touchline and caught sight of Archie's wonder goal diagram. He'd intended to stay where he was in case Weldon got the ball and mounted a counter-attack but, seeing the diagram, he decided to go forward. There was no point in being defensive now. There could only be seconds left. He trotted towards the Weldon penalty area.

Archie, meanwhile, had taken up a position in the middle of the goal ready to rush out and stop any pushes or prods that the Weldon defenders might be planning – particularly on Rollo. They knew that he was the main threat and already three of them had gathered around the tall striker, ready to stop him from getting to the cross that would surely come . . .

But Sam didn't cross the ball. Cleverly, she pushed it out towards Zak, who was standing on the edge of the box unmarked. It was a great ball, but as Zak prepared to shoot, Ricky suddenly slid in to him. The Weldon captain whammed into Zak's leg with a sickening thud. Both players went down.

The ball rolled into the arc of the penalty box just as Dan arrived. Without hesitation, he swung his foot and struck it mightily. It was one of the cleanest shots he'd ever kicked. The ball flew by the crowd of players in the box and

rocketed into the top corner of the Weldon net. The goalie didn't even move. In fact, for an instant, no one moved. Players, spectators, managers – even the referee – seemed in a state of shock.

At last, the referee blew his whistle and a huge cheer went up from the touchline as the Leggs United supporters acclaimed their team's equalizer. But even then Dan didn't celebrate: he was worried about Zak, who was still lying where he had fallen. Dan ran over to his friend.

"Zak," Dan called anxiously. "Are you OK?"

Zak rolled over to face Dan. His large brown eyes sparkled. "I'm fine," he said happily. He nodded at Ricky, who was rolling on the grass nearby, holding his foot and wincing. "I reckon Archie's shin-guard did the trick," Zak laughed and he glanced across at the phantom manager, who was leaning against one of the goalposts, shimmering with satisfaction. Zak turned to Dan once more. "Cool goal," he said admiringly.

"Thanks," said Dan and then, finally, it sank in: the score was 2–2. Leggs United had equalized with the last kick of the match – and it was *his* goal that had saved the day!

Chapter Thirteen

AN HONOURABLE DRAW

"OK, OK," said Sam nonchalantly. "So you scored one lucky goal. Big deal." She picked a blade of grass and shielded her eyes against the bright morning sun.

"Lucky!" Dan protested. "It was a brilliant strike." He drew back his foot and mimed the shot that had brought the equalizer against Weldon Wanderers the previous afternoon. He kicked so hard that his trainer flew off, sailed through the air and flopped on to the pitch. Sam and Zak laughed as Dan hopped after it. "It *was* a good goal, though, wasn't it?" he said, slipping his trainer back on.

"It was great," Zak assured him. He nodded his head and black ringlets of hair swayed across his eyes.

"It was all right," Sam conceded grudgingly. "It was my corner that set it up, though."

"And my pass," Zak added.

"That wasn't a pass," Sam scoffed, wrinkling her freckly nose. "You were tackled."

"Well, it ended up as a good pass anyway," said Dan. He thought for a moment. "It was a brilliant team effort," he concluded.

"Yeah," Zak agreed. Then he grinned. "I'm glad Archie gave me that shin-guard," he said.

"Me too," said Sam. The eyes of all three children focused on the old ball, lying on the ground in front of them. "Shall I call him?" Sam asked.

Dan nodded. "Go on," he said.

Sam picked up the old ball and went throught her familiar calling-up-Archie routine. She rubbed the ball gently and wailed, "Arise, O Archie. Archie, arise."

The children were expecting the phantom footballer to fizz out of the ball like a

firecracker. But he didn't. What came out was a sort of pale mist.

"Archie?" said Sam questioningly.

And then, at last, Archie did appear, materializing from inside the mist. He was very faint, though – and quite transparent in the bright sunlight. He barely glowed at all.

"Are you all right, Archie?" Dan asked with concern.

Archie's oddly colourless eyebrows met in a deep glare. "Of course I'm not all right," he growled. "You disturbed me from my sleep. I was having a particularly good dream too – I was refereeing the cup final." His eyebrows parted, as his face relaxed into a smile. "I was making an excellent job of it too," he continued, "though I say it myself."

The three children threw back their heads and groaned.

The conversation quickly turned to the match against Weldon. In the end a draw was a good result, they all agreed. At half-time, after all, Leggs United had seemed dead and buried. Archie, however, claimed that the second-half turnaround came as no surprise.

"Let me tell you something particularly wise and original that Herbert Chapman once said on the subject," he pronounced grandly. "He said – and I quote – 'Football is a game of two halves.' " He beamed, inviting appreciation for his hero's brilliance.

The children's reaction, however, was not what Archie expected. They burst out laughing.

"But, Archie," Sam giggled, "that's not original. Everyone says that."

Archie frowned woozily. "Do they?" he muttered. "Well, er, maybe everyone does say that *now*. But Herbert Chapman said it first."

He waggled his walrus moustache emphatically. "Anyway," he went on, "my point is that in the first half of the game, the present, in the shape of Weldon Wanderers, may have come out on top, but in the second, the past and the spirit of the great Herbert Chapman were unquestionably the victors."

"Those old shin-guards certainly came out on top," Zak remarked. "That Ricky was hopping about like he'd kicked a postbox."

Archie tutted with disapproval. "In my day," he sniffed, "that ruffian would not have lasted two minutes. The referee was much too lenient. That's why I had to take matters into my own hands."

"You said you didn't like referees interfering," said Sam pointedly, running her hand over her short red hair.

"Ah, yes, well . . ." Archie appeared flustered for an instant. But he quickly recovered his composure. "When the play is fair, the referee should be invisible," he stated coolly, raising one fuzzy finger. "But when the play is foul, he should intervene and take strong action. That referee failed to do his duty."

"You're right there," said Dan. "That first half was like the Battle of Highbury."

"Indeed," said Archie gravely. "And in a battle, you must have protection. Hence, the shin-guards."

"Yes, well, I've learnt my lesson," said Sam. "I'll wear shin-pads in future. But not those old ones – they were too big. I couldn't play a whole game in *those*."

Archie tutted once more. "As I told you before," he said with a shake of his head, "the great Cliff Bastin managed perfectly well."

"But he was a grown-up!" Sam exclaimed.

"When I first saw him play," sniffed Archie, "he was just a slip of a lad – not much bigger than you."

Sam glanced at Dan and rolled her eyes.

Zak, however, was looking at Archie with real interest. "I've heard of Cliff Bastin," he said brightly.

Archie beamed at his young relative. "Ah, so the legend does endure," he purred.

"He was Arsenal's record goal-scorer," Zak added, showing once again his impressive knowledge of football facts.

"Another victory for the past, it seems," Archie commented smugly.

"Well, not exactly," said Zak and the others all stared at him. "He *was* the record goal-scorer," Zak explained, "but he's not any more. Ian Wright is."

Archie flickered with confusion. "And *who* is Ian Wright?" he boomed.

"He's a player from our day, the present," said Sam with a cheeky grin.

Archie looked deeply perplexed. He seemed fuzzier than ever.

"Well," said Dan, pulling at his ear, "I think football was great in the past and football's great in the present. You can't say which one's better."

Sam and Zak muttered agreement and even Archie nodded his head appreciatively. "Well said, laddy," he murmured. His face relaxed into a warm, hazy smile. "We shall call it an honourable draw . . ."

Up for the Cup

To Josie,
my great entertainer

Chapter One
EXCITING NEWS

"Tottenham!" Sam Legg screeched. "We've drawn Tottenham Hotspur! At home!" She danced about the sitting room as if her team, Muddington Rovers, had *won* the cup rather than just being drawn against a top Premier League team in round three.

Her older brother, Dan Legg, was excited too. He sat on the sofa with a broad grin on his round, freckly face. "Tottenham Hotspur, at home," he repeated dreamily. It seemed almost too good to be true. Suddenly, his grin slipped into an anxious frown. "Do you think we'll get tickets?" he said, tugging at his ear.

"You bet!" declared Sam. "I wouldn't miss this match for the world." She tossed her head emphatically. "Anyway," she added, "Dad says that people who turn up to support regularly go to the front of the queue for cup tickets."

Sam and Dan often went to see Muddington Rovers play. Usually they went with their dad, Stephen Legg, and their younger twin brothers, Giles and Justin. Sometimes their cousin Zak Browne, Dan's best friend, went too. He lived in the same street as Sam and Dan; a third set of cousins lived in the house next door to them. The children of all three families were football mad and had formed a team called Leggs United.

"We'll have to get Archie to come too," said Sam, running her hand over her short red hair.

"Yeah, well, it's easy for him, isn't it?" said Dan. "He doesn't need a ticket."

Archie, alias Archibald Legg, was the

children's great-great-uncle, deceased. He had once been a player for Muddington Rovers, but, after being struck down by lightning, he had become a ghost. For over sixty years, he had been trapped inside an old ball in the Leggs' loft, until, quite by chance, Sam and Dan had released him. Now he was the manager of Leggs United.

"Let's call him up and tell him the great news," said Sam.

"Good idea," Dan agreed.

The two children went over to the glass-fronted cabinet which housed the old football, flanked by a pair of ancient leather shin-guards. Sam lifted the ball out and started to rub it gently. Then, as if she were Aladdin summoning the genie from his magic lamp, she wailed, "Archie. Arise, O Archie!"

Her words had an immediate and dramatic effect. There was a fizz and a flash and a ghostly figure whooshed out of the ball into the room. He stood, shimmering and sparkling from head to toe like tinsel on a Christmas tree.

For a moment, the two children stared at the phantom footballer, taking in the knotted red neckerchief, the old black and green striped Muddington Rovers shirt, the long, baggy, white shorts, the thick green socks that concealed bulky shin-pads and the clumpy leather football boots with steel toecaps. As ever, Archie's skin was almost transparently pale and contrasted with the bright red of his bushy caterpillar eyebrows, enormous walrus moustache and flaming shock of hair. Around him there was a ghostly glow.

"Mmm, I feel in fine fettle," he announced, with an extravagant waggle of his moustache. "That new contraption of your mother's is really most invigorating."

"Eh?" Dan uttered, puzzled.

"Archie charged himself up on Mum's new sewing machine," Sam explained, giggling. "Mum was making one of her dresses at the time, right. Suddenly the machine went completely crazy and Mum stitched the dress material to the sleeve of her jumper. She was really mad."

"Yes, well, just a minor accident," Archie burbled. "These things happen with electricity." Archie had discovered that if he focused on something electrical, it boosted his ghostly energy. Right now he was ablaze with it. "In my day, of course," he went on, "we relied a lot more on gas. Gas, you know, is far more dependable . . ."

Dan quickly interrupted before Archie could launch into one of his lectures about the old days. "Archie, we've got something important to tell you," he cried. "Muddington Rovers have drawn Tottenham Hotspur in the cup!"

Archie showed no excitement. In fact, he met the news with a look of cool disdain. "Tottenham, eh?" he sniffed. "Well, Muddington should make mincemeat of a minor team like that."

Sam and Dan stared at Archie once more, this time in total astonishment.

"Tottenham aren't minor," said Dan at last. "They're one of the biggest clubs in the country."

Now it was Archie's turn to show astonishment. "Tottenham, a big club?" he queried. "Why, in my day, they were a very minor outfit indeed. They weren't even in the top division." He paused an instant, raising his thick eyebrows. "But then, of course, in my day every club was minor compared to the great Herbert Chapman's Arsenal."

Sam and Dan looked at one another and rolled their eyes. Archie was always going on about the Arsenal side of the 1930s and its manager, Herbert Chapman. If he'd mentioned them once, he'd mentioned them a thousand times.

"Well, anyway, Archie," Dan said, changing the subject back to the present, "Tottenham are a very big team now."

"But Muddington Rovers are still going to beat them," said Sam with a defiant toss of her head. "Tommy Banks will tear them apart."

"Mmm, well, strange things happen in the cup, laddy," Archie stated calmly. Usually Sam corrected Archie when he

called her "laddy", but right now she was too busy dreaming of her hero, Tommy Banks, Muddington Rovers' star striker. "Tell me," continued Archie, "when is this great match to take place?"

"The day after our cup match against Amberley Park," Dan informed his ghostly relative. The cup in question was the Muddington District Junior Cup. Amberley Park were Leggs United's opponents in the first round.

“We’ll thrash them,” Sam chirped and she started dancing around the room again.

Archie shook his head and sighed.

Chapter Two

MOUNTAINS AND MOLEHILLS

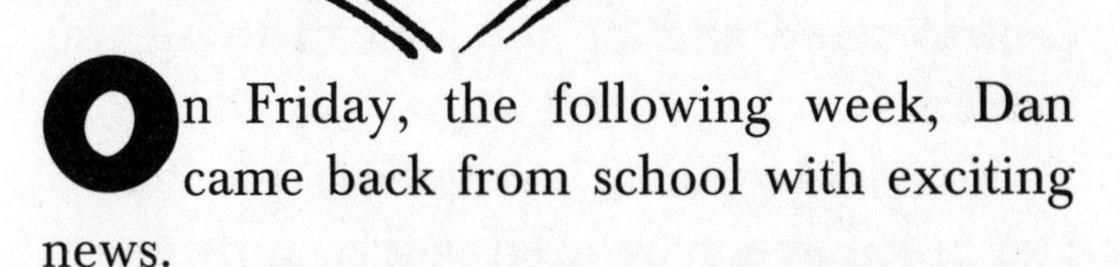

On Friday, the following week, Dan came back from school with exciting news.

"I'm going to the match!" he cried, bursting into the kitchen, where his family were about to eat their tea.

"That's nice, dear," said Ann Legg, putting a plate of hot crumpets on the table. "Which match is that?"

"The cup match!" Dan exclaimed. "Muddington against Tottenham. We're going to be guests of honour. Mr Barnard said."

Mr Barnard was the teacher in charge of Muddington Primary's school football team. At the end of football practice that afternoon, as Dan now explained, he had given his team the news that they had all been invited to the cup match against Tottenham. They were going as the special guests of Muddington Rovers' new chairman, who was an old boy of Muddington Primary. They'd watch the game from the hospitality seats in the central stand and be introduced to all the players.

"You lucky devil," said Sam enviously. Her green eyes narrowed in a grumpy glare. "It's not fair. I should go too."

"But you're not in the team," Dan reminded her.

"I ought to be," Sam grumbled. It was a rule at Muddington Primary that only children in the top class could play for the school team.

"Well, you will be next year," said Ann Legg soothingly.

"But that's no good, is it?" Sam

complained. "I want to be in the team now and meet the Muddington players with Dan and Zak and Zoe." Zak Browne and Zoe Legg were both in the top class like Dan and played for the school team.

"I'll get you Tommy Banks's autograph," Dan offered.

But Sam was not pacified. "Hmph," she grunted, wrinkling her small nose disgustedly.

She was still sulking the next day when Leggs United gathered for their Saturday morning training session with Archie. There were a couple of things he wanted to sort out before their league match that afternoon against Marchmont Road Juniors.

It was Leggs United's first ever season in the Muddington Junior League, a local football league for under-twelves. So far they were doing well and had won most of their matches. They'd already played Marchmont Road Juniors away and beaten them, so they expected to win the return game at home.

Leggs United's home ground was a

meadow, at the bottom of the gardens of No. 15 and No. 17 Poplar Street, owned by the Legg family. They played all their home matches there and they trained there too. The meadow had been turned into a football pitch during the last week of the summer holidays by the Leggs and Brownes themselves – under the critical eye of Archie. The phantom coach was always quick to point out any fault he found with the playing surface.

He was standing now in the centre circle,

frowning at a bump on the pitch. It looked suspiciously like a molehill.

"Moles," he tutted. "What confounded creatures they are."

His remark drew an immediate reaction from Sam. "I think they're nice," she retorted fiercely.

"Only because they're small and chubby and they remind you of Tommy Banks," teased Dan.

Sam gave her older brother a scorching look.

"Tommy Banks isn't small or chubby," she hissed. "He's well built with a low centre of gravity, like lots of great players."

"Very true, very true," Archie agreed. "Take Alex James, the great Arsenal playmaker, for example."

"And Maradona," said Zak, who knew a lot about football facts and figures. "He was short and stocky and my dad says he was the best player in the world when Argentina last won the World Cup."

"Indeed," said Archie. He wrinkled his enormous moustache. "However, that still doesn't make me think any better of moles . . . To me they are like bad referees."

"Moles aren't like referees!" the twins exclaimed together.

"Indeed they are," Archie corrected them.

"But how?" Dan enquired.

"Well," said Archie, "they are blind, useless and a menace to all around them."

Most of the children laughed, but Sam screwed up her freckly nose in distaste.

"Well, I think, Archie," she said sharply, "that you're making a mountain out of a molehill."

"Ah, you won't say that when this whole pitch is covered in bumps," Archie insisted, "and the ball is bobbling about like a buoy in a hurricane." He raised one pale, bony finger. "No, if this continues, something will have to be done. We cannot have our cup match ruined by a bumpy playing field."

"We could get them with our catapults," Giles suggested.

"Yes," added Justin. "Or with my super-soaker water gun."

“Don’t you dare!” said Sam angrily. “You leave them alone.” She glowered at the twins, then turned towards Archie and Dan, both of whom were smiling. “I think you’re horrible!” she exploded. Then she stormed away across the meadow.

Chapter Three

SAM IN A SULK

The match against Marchmont Road Juniors turned out to be harder than Leggs United had anticipated. The visitors had acquired some good players since the teams had last played and they were much stronger. In addition, with Sam still sulking and hardly getting involved in the game at all, Leggs United were a lot weaker. At half-time, the score was nil–all, but Marchmont had had the better chances. Two fine saves by Gabby and a header off the line by Dan were all that had kept the scoresheet blank.

During the half-time break, Sam refused

to speak to anyone. She sat on her own away from the rest of the team. She wouldn't even talk to her mum or dad.

"Come on, Sam, this is stupid," Dan pleaded, but Sam ignored him.

"Leave her be, laddy," Archie advised. "She'll come round." Herbert Chapman, Archie told his captain, had had countless rows with his great playmaker, Alex James, but it had always worked out all right in the end. On one occasion before an important cup tie, he recalled, the great manager had had to haul his star player out of bed to get him to play. "But patience is a great virtue in these instances," he declared with a small twitch of his moustache.

Dan's patience with his sister was sorely tried in the second half. She didn't like tackling at the best of times, but against Marchmont she made no attempt at all to win the ball. Time after time the opposing midfield players ran past her unchallenged. Dan and his fellow defenders had to work really hard to cover for her.

What really annoyed Dan, though, was

that even when he gave Sam the ball, she didn't use it properly. Normally, she was brilliant on the ball: she dribbled past opponents and passed cleverly. She was, in Archie's words, "the fulcrum of the team", the creator of most of Leggs United's attacks.

There was one move in particular that Archie liked to employ. It was based on a classic Arsenal tactic devised by Herbert Chapman, in which the ball was moved from defence to midfield to the wing and back in to the central striker in a matter of seconds. Leggs United had used the tactic successfully often in their matches so far. But in the game against Marchmont, the move never got going, thanks to Sam. In fact she didn't play a decent pass in the whole match. She kept trying to run with the ball on her own.

Finally, with a quarter of an hour left, matters came to a head. Dan passed the ball to Sam just outside his own penalty area and, half-heartedly, she tried to go past two opponents. They robbed her easily and bore down on the Leggs United goal. Dan and his defenders were outnumbered. The ball was passed among the attacking Marchmont players and found one of their strikers unmarked on the edge of the six-yard box. Fortunately for Leggs United, his shot was a bad one. The ball seemed to take a bobble as he hit it and his shot rolled against the post and behind for a goal kick.

Dan was furious. "Look, if you're going to give the ball away like that, you might as well get off the pitch!" he shouted at Sam, his round face red with anger.

Sam glared back. "OK then, I will!" she shouted. "See how you get on without me." She turned and started to walk from the pitch.

In a flash, Archie was there beside her. "Come on, laddy – I mean lassy," he quickly corrected himself. "You can't desert your team now. They need you."

"No they don't," Sam retorted sharply. "Dan just said so."

"You mustn't take to heart what's said in the heat of the moment," Archie persisted, flashing his young relative a gleaming smile. He flourished his moustache indulgently. "Why, I remember the Arsenal skipper, Herbie Roberts, giving Alex James a terrible earful and . . ."

But Sam butted in before he could get any further. "I don't give a stuff about your old players, Archie," she snapped harshly. "I'm not playing any more and that's final."

And, for the second time that day, she stormed from the meadow.

Chapter Four

GRUMPS AND GRUDGES

Somehow, through desperate defending and a piece of skilful finishing by Zak, a ten-man Leggs United managed to beat Marchmont by one goal to nil. However, the atmosphere at No. 15 Poplar Street, in the days that followed, was far from happy. Dan and Sam were not speaking to one another – and if Sam spoke to anyone else it was usually with a grunt or a snarl.

Sam was especially snappy with the twins, whose latest hobby, playing the recorder, was driving her crazy. Dan had some sympathy with her over this: he found their playing unbearable too. It wasn't just that they were very bad and very loud, it was that they each played a different tune. The cacophony that came from their room was ten times worse than an alley full of fighting tomcats. It certainly did nothing to improve harmony in the Legg household.

Ann and Stephen Legg did their best to smooth things over, so too did Zak, but without success. Dan was willing to make

up with his sister if she made the first move, but there seemed no chance of that. Sam was set into a major sulk.

She wasn't the only one either. Archie was also in a grump. When Dan summoned him from the ball, he smouldered and flickered like hot ashes. He would not speak to Sam, he said, until she apologized to him for her rudeness.

"Herbert Chapman was never treated like this," he declared moodily.

"But I thought you said he often had rows with Alex James," Dan reminded his ghostly ancestor.

"Ah, yes, well," Archie mumbled, "that was different. Alex James was a great star. Your sister's . . . well . . ." He wrinkled his moustache critically. "She's just a temperamental . . . girl."

"Don't I know it," sighed Dan bitterly. He was glad, though, that Sam wasn't in the room to hear Archie's remark. Sparks really would have flown.

It was a difficult few days for Leggs United. The feud between Sam and Dan and Archie disrupted the team's preparations for their important cup match against Amberley Park. Archie refused to hold any training sessions until everything was sorted out. He wouldn't even discuss tactics with his team.

"But, Archie, you're our coach," Dan protested, "and this is our biggest match yet. We need you."

"Coach I may be, whipping boy I am not," Archie sniffed. "You can tell your sister that."

Dan looked at his phantom relative in bewilderment. "But I don't even know what it means," he said, tugging at one ear.

Archie drew himself up and glowered at his captain. "It means that I will not be spoken to as your sister spoke to me," he pronounced huffily. Then, quick as a mole down a hole, he vanished into the old ball.

The following afternoon, after school, Dan and Zak went down to the meadow to practise. It seemed odd, though, not having Sam there too. Dan even missed her jibes about his shooting ability. The truth was, he wasn't the sort to hold grudges and his anger with Sam soon passed. He actually felt quite sorry for her. It was a shame that she wasn't going with him and his cousins to meet the Muddington Rovers players – especially as she was such a big fan of Tommy Banks.

By Tuesday evening, he decided that something just had to be done.

"We can't let this go on any longer," he told Zak, as the two of them walked back from the meadow. "We've got to get Archie and Sam talking to one another again or we won't be properly prepared for Saturday's match."

"But how are we going to do that?" Zak asked, his face hidden behind curly strands of black hair.

"I don't know," Dan confessed with a sigh, "but if Sam's still sulking when I get back from school tomorrow, then I'm going up to her room and I'm not going to leave until she's seen sense." He frowned grimly and, remembering Archie's story about Herbert Chapman hauling Alex James out of bed, he added decisively, "I'm going to get her back out on the pitch, even if I have to drag her!"

Chapter Five

MR BARNARD'S BOMBSHELL

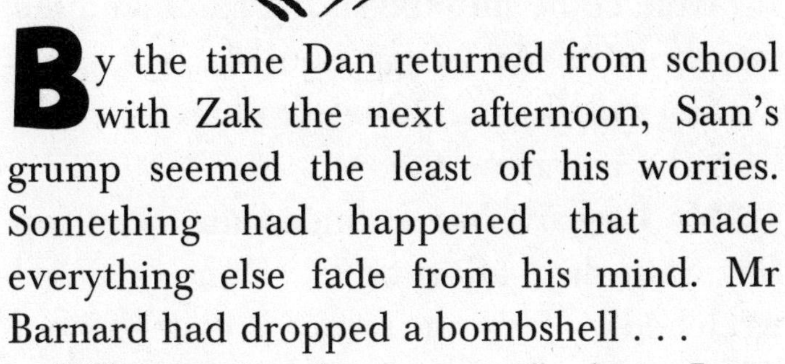

By the time Dan returned from school with Zak the next afternoon, Sam's grump seemed the least of his worries. Something had happened that made everything else fade from his mind. Mr Barnard had dropped a bombshell . . .

"Whatever's the matter?" Ann Legg asked, seeing the look of dejection on Dan and Zak's faces. "You two look awful."

"We've had some bad news," said Dan.

"Terrible," sighed Zak. The two boys dropped their sports bags on the hall floor, as if they were discarding all hope.

"Well, come into the sitting room and tell me about it," Ann Legg cajoled.

Dan called up Archie, so that he could hear the bad news too.

"Mr Barnard has arranged an away trip for Saturday afternoon," Dan revealed wretchedly. "It's at some private school down near the coast. Apparently the football teacher there is a friend of his. He had a little tournament planned, but one of the teams had to pull out at the last moment, so he asked Mr Barnard if Muddington Primary would step in." Dan scowled. "I reckon old Barnard only wants to go to show off to his mate about going to the cup game against Tottenham."

Archie peered at Dan with a puzzled air. "This is all very interesting," he muttered, "but I fail to see the problem. You are already playing in a match on Saturday against Amberley Park. Your Mr Barnyard–"

"Barnard," Dan corrected him.

"Your Mr Barnard," Archie continued, "will simply have to replace you and Zak and Zoe with three reserves."

Dan and Zak looked at each other and sighed. "It's not that simple, Archie," Dan informed his phantom ancestor. "We told Barnard about our game, didn't we, Zak?"

Zak nodded in a flurry of ringlets. "We did," he confirmed. "He said we had to play. The school comes first, he said."

"If we don't play, we can't go to the match on Sunday," Dan added glumly.

"Well, that's not right," said Ann Legg sharply. "I'll have a word with him."

But Dan quickly shook his head. "There's no point, Mum," he said hopelessly. "He won't change his mind. He never does."

"Even when he's totally wrong," Zak remarked with unusual bite.

"Like now," said Dan.

"Hmm," Archie muttered with deep disapproval. "He sounds like a very poor manager indeed. The ability to admit one's mistakes is an essential requirement of good management."

The two children looked a little quizzically at their own manager: they'd never heard him admit he was wrong about anything.

"He isn't a good manager," said Dan. He shrugged, then tugged disconsolately at his ear. "But that's not the point. He's *our* manager and what he says goes." He puffed out his round cheeks with a resigned air. "So either we play for Leggs United against Amberley Park and don't go to the match against Tottenham and meet all the Muddington Rovers players . . ." He paused and sighed. "Or we don't play against Amberley, go with the school team on Saturday instead and see the match on Sunday."

"A dilemma indeed," Archie mused, caressing his moustache with great care.

"Well, we've already decided what we're going to do, haven't we, Zak?" Dan said gloomily.

Zak nodded. "We talked about it on the way home from school," he said.

"What *are* you going to do?" Ann Legg enquired.

"We're going to play against Amberley Park, of course," Dan replied limply. "We couldn't let our family down."

It was a noble gesture, but neither Zak or Dan looked any the better for making it. In football-speak, they looked as sick as parrots.

"Well," Dan continued wearily, "I guess I'd better go and talk to Sam. At least she's got one less reason to be grumpy with me now, hasn't she?" He smiled grimly, but as he walked out of the room, his eyes were near to tears.

Chapter Six
LEGGS REUNITED!

Dan knocked on Sam's door, his spirits drooping even further as he read the handwritten sign that hung from the door: *No boys allowed. Keep out! By order. Sam.*

"Who is it?" came the sharp response from the other side of the door.

"It's me, Dan," said Dan softly. "I want to talk to you."

"Well, I don't want to talk to you," Sam retorted sharply. "Go away."

Dan opened the door anyway.

"I said go away!" Sam hissed as Dan walked into her room. Dan stood by the door and gazed in at his sister. She was lying on her bed, reading a football magazine. Next to her on the wall was a huge, full-colour poster of Tommy Banks.

"I'm not going away, Sam," Dan insisted. "Not until we've talked."

Sam sighed heavily and shrugged. "Go on, then," she said coolly. "What have you got to say?"

Dan pulled at his ear tensely. "Well, first, I wanted to say sorry," he began, "for shouting at you in the match on Saturday."

"Huh," Sam grunted. She scowled at the magazine in front of her.

"Sam," Dan pleaded, "we've got to all pull together, otherwise we'll never have a chance against Amberley. We'll go out of the cup in the first round."

"I don't care," Sam growled. But Dan knew she did really. She wanted Leggs United to do well in the cup more than anybody. He suddenly felt a surge of anger: he'd had enough of all this.

"Look, Sam, I'm giving up going to the Tottenham match to play against

Amberley," he exploded. "The least you can do is make up with me and Archie."

Sam was about to respond, then stopped. She stared at Dan quizzically.

"What do you mean, you're giving up the Tottenham match?" she asked.

Dan explained about Mr Barnard's bombshell and what he and Zak had decided to do.

"That's so unfair," Sam said, her own grievances forgotten now. "He can't stop you from going to the match."

"He can," Dan answered miserably. "He has."

He looked so downcast that Sam searched desperately for something to say that might cheer him up. "You could sit with us," she suggested tentatively. "Dad'll get you tickets."

But Dan shook his head. "There aren't any tickets left now," he replied unhappily. "The game's sold out – I heard them say so on the radio this morning."

Now Sam's face fell too. "I'm sorry, Dan," she said.

"Yeah," Dan grunted. He looked down at the floor, his throat tightening, and breathed deeply.

When he felt calmer, he turned again to the reason he'd come to Sam's room. "So . . . you'll play on Saturday? Properly, I mean. You'll be our fulcrum again. Our Alex James."

Sam smiled. "The great Alex James!" she declared in a voice that imitated Archie. Then she and Dan both laughed.

"Archie's still sulking, you know," Dan said. "He hasn't forgiven you for telling him to stuff his old players. He's taken it as a personal insult."

Sam wrinkled her small nose. "I didn't mean it like that," she said. "I was just angry, that's all."

"I know," said Dan. "But could you tell Archie that? We need him to start coaching us again. Things are getting really desperate."

Sam flicked back her fringe and nodded. "Oh, OK," she sighed.

"He's downstairs now, with Zak," Dan

said. He glanced at the door to suggest they go and see. Sam put down her magazine and rolled off the bed. As she did so, a terrible squeaking started up along the landing. The twins had begun their evening recorder practice.

Sam and Dan looked at one another and shook their heads, wincing at the awful combination of Hot Cross Buns and Jingle Bells.

They found Archie, with his foot on the old ball, in the middle of a story about an ancient FA Cup Final. He glanced towards

Sam and Dan as they entered the room, but continued with his tale. As ever it involved Herbert Chapman. He was manager of Huddersfield Town at the time, apparently, and they were playing Preston in the final.

"As I was saying," Archie intoned, with a nod at Zak, "it was a dreadfully dull match until the 67th minute, when Huddersfield were awarded a penalty. Hamilton, the Preston full-back, brought down Billy Smith, the Huddersfield winger, on the edge of the penalty area. But was it inside or outside? Most people thought the latter, but the referee disagreed. 'Penalty!' he said."

Archie paused for a moment and, though he ignored Dan and Sam, Dan could tell he was pleased that his audience had now trebled in size. "The goalkeeper was one JF Mitchell," Archie continued with a disapproving twitch of his great moustache, "and he danced about on his line like an excited monkey begging for peanuts. It was quite ridiculous." His hairy eyebrows met in an upside-down V.

"I've heard of him," Zak said.

"Indeed?" Archie queried with a gratified smile.

"He's the only goalie to wear glasses in a cup final," Zak stated proudly.

"Quite right," Archie congratulated his young relative, "he did wear glasses. But he didn't save the penalty. Smith scored and Huddersfield won the cup." Archie beamed at the memory.

"Another great day for Herbert Chapman, eh?" Dan ventured lightly.

Archie looked at Dan. "A good day certainly," he agreed. "Though, of course, his best days were yet to come."

"At Arsenal," Zak affirmed.

"Precisely," Archie nodded.

"With Alex James," Sam interjected. Then, having got the phantom coach's attention, she added quickly, "I'm sorry for what I said the other day, Archie. Really I am. I was angry with Dan, not you. I know Alex James was a great player."

"Hmm," Archie muttered. His eyebrows hopped and his moustache wiggled, as he regarded his young playmaker. "Well, apology accepted," he declared at last. "Now we can commence with planning our own cup victory – once we've sorted out this other unfortunate matter, of course . . ."

Sam's eyes sparked with outrage. "It's not right!" she cried suddenly. She gestured towards Dan and Zak. "You were invited to the Tottenham match. You should be allowed to go."

"Try telling old Barnard that," Dan commented bitterly.

There was silence for a moment, then Archie gave a small cough. In the twilight, his ghostly figure gleamed and shimmered. "Well," he announced decisively, "that is precisely what I intend to do."

Chapter Seven
GHOST AT SCHOOL

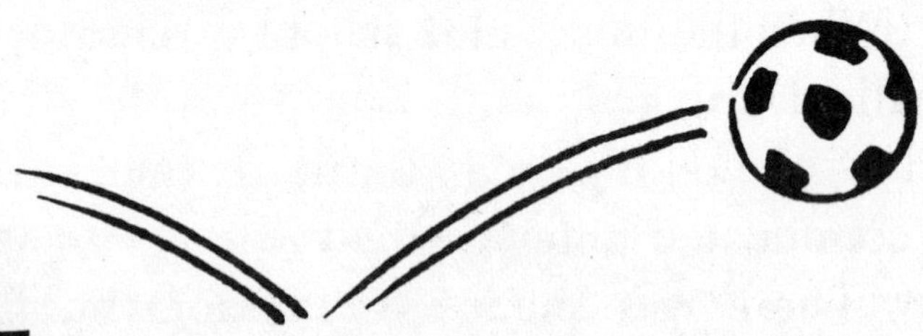

The next morning, Archie accompanied the children to school.

"But, Archie," Dan protested, "Mr Barnard won't be able to hear you if you do talk to him."

Archie, it had been established, was only visible and audible to his own family – a state of affairs that had already caused him much frustration. Today, however, he was nonchalance itself, as he floated along the street, his outline glowing brightly.

"Ah, trust me," he said mysteriously, tapping one bony finger to his nose. "We spirits have ways of making ourselves understood."

"If you say so," Dan said with a despondent air. He didn't hold out much hope that Archie would be successful. He felt doomed to missing out on being a guest of honour at the Tottenham match.

When they arrived at school, Archie went with Dan, Zak and Zoe towards their classroom.

"Good luck," Sam called as they walked away.

"Luck?" Archie retorted with an extravagant waggle of his huge moustache. "Who needs luck, laddy, when you have genius?"

Sam smiled and shook her head. "I hope you're right, Archie," she said to herself.

As he floated through the school, Archie had plenty to say about what he saw around him. For a start, there was the uniform. When he was a lad, he remarked, ties and blazers were obligatory – he didn't approve of the sweatshirts and tracksuit trousers that many of the children wore. But it was their shoes that drew his greatest criticism.

"In my day," he stated sternly, "you could see your face in your shoes, they were so shiny." He glanced down proudly at the gleaming toecaps of his own size-twelve boots. "I always kept my footwear in immaculate condition," he added, looking pointedly at Dan's shoes, which were scuffed and dull.

"My dad polishes my shoes once a week," Dan said defensively.

"Once a week, laddy!" Archie exclaimed. "Shoes should be polished every day. You should treat them like you treat your pet rabbit."

"But I don't have a pet rabbit," Dan replied, bemused.

"Well, all the more reason to look after your shoes," Archie insisted.

But if he was critical of the pupils' dress, Archie was horrified at their teachers' appearance.

"Why, I've seen smarter tramps," he sniffed disgustedly as they passed a group of teachers in the corridor. The children burst out laughing – then quickly had to pretend they were coughing when the teachers glared at them.

They came at last to the top classroom. Dan, Zak and Zoe sat at their tables, while Archie prowled about the room peering reproachfully about him. When Mr Barnard came in, Archie fixed him with a steely gaze.

"So this is your manager," he observed dismissively.

As the teacher read the register, Archie wandered to the front of the class. He studied Mr Barnard closely. "Well, at least he's wearing a jacket and tie," he commented. He ran one finger lightly across the teacher's collar. "Limp," he scolded. "Not nearly enough starch."

Mr Barnard paused and glanced up from his book with a puzzled expression. He waggled his neck as if to get rid of some minor irritation.

Zak and Zoe stared at Archie goggle-eyed, while Dan frowned and shook his head vigorously.

"Is something the matter, Daniel?" Mr Barnard demanded sharply.

Dan froze. "No, sir," he muttered. "My neck was just a bit stiff."

"Mmm," the teacher murmured. "I trust it'll unstiffen by Saturday. You are coming with us on Saturday, aren't you?" He gave Dan a piercing look.

Dan's head bowed; his heart thumped in his chest. "No, sir," he said quietly.

"No?" Mr Barnard queried. His small, deep-set eyes bored into Dan, who shuffled on his chair uneasily.

"I can't go on the school trip, sir," Dan explained. "I've got to play for Leggs United."

"Really?" Mr Barnard snorted. "And what about you, Zak? And Zoe?"

The two children shook their heads. "We have to play for Leggs United too," Zak said.

"Very well. But you know the consequences," Mr Barnard informed them. "If you don't come with the team on Saturday, you don't come on Sunday either." He raised his hands. "Right, that's my last word on the subject. Now, let's get on." He picked up his pen to continue, but Archie tapped it from his fingers. The pen rolled across the teacher's desk and clattered on to the floor.

"Now, just a minute, sir," Archie remonstrated. He loomed over Mr Barnard like a huge flame. "This matter is far from closed. These lads are playing for me on Saturday and you have no right to punish them." He raised a finger like a referee giving a caution. "I demand that you reverse your decision," he boomed.

It was an impressive performance, but

wasted of course. Mr Barnard neither saw nor heard Archie. He picked up his pen and, after studying it a moment, he completed the register.

"Right, class, maths books out," he ordered.

But Archie was far from finished. When Mr Barnard got up and began to walk around the tables, Archie sat down in his seat and started writing. When Mr Barnard returned to his desk, he looked down and frowned. Waves of deep wrinkles appeared on his large forehead and his eyes looked hostile.

"Daniel," he said. "I presume this is your work." He held up a piece of paper and read it out: "*Dan, Zak and Zoe must be allowed to play for Leggs United on Saturday without penalty. Signed, Archibald Legg, the Phantom of the Cup.*"

"The Phantom of the Cup," Mr Barnard repeated tartly. He glared at Dan. "Save your imagination for creative writing, Daniel. Any more nonsense like this and I shall put you in detention this lunchtime."

"But it wasn't me, sir," Dan complained.

"Oh, I suppose it really was a ghost, was it?" Mr Barnard mocked.

Dan's body sagged. What was the point of trying to explain? Mr Barnard would never believe him.

Archie attempted to come to his young relative's assistance.

"Leave the boy be," he rebuked, his eyes ablaze. "It was I, Archibald Legg, who wrote the note." As before, however, his words fell on deaf ears.

For a while, Archie retreated to the windowsill, where he perched like some massive bird, deep in thought. But he was determined to make himself "heard", and he was soon up on his feet again.

His next trick was truly spectacular. While Mr Barnard was rummaging in a big storage cupboard and the children were busy with their maths, Archie picked up a piece of chalk and started writing on the blackboard, repeating his earlier message.

Gradually faces started to turn towards the blackboard and an astonished gasp went round the room at the sight of a piece of chalk writing on its own.

Mr Barnard was the last to witness Archie's display. He appeared from the cupboard with a box of maths puzzles, just as Archie was signing his name. The teacher gaped, eyes boggling, for an instant, his face draining of colour. He swallowed so hard that his Adam's apple bounced in his throat. The box of puzzles dropped from his hands and spilled noisily across the floor . . .

The racket seemed to snap him out of his stupor. He turned to Dan with a furious expression.

"I don't know how you did that, Daniel," he thundered, "but you can spend your lunch hour in here, writing that message until you're as sick of the sight of it as I am!"

Dan closed his eyes in silent misery. Archie's antics had made things much worse, not better. The situation was hopeless.

Chapter Eight

BAD NEWS AND GOOD

Dan was the picture of gloom that afternoon as he told his family about his disastrous day at school – and Archie's part in it.

"Where is Archie?" Sam asked when he'd finished.

Dan shrugged. "Back in his ball, I suppose," he said. "He disappeared at the end of school."

"He's probably too embarrassed to show his face," Ann Legg remarked drily, "after the mess he seems to have made of things." She ruffled Dan's hair comfortingly. "This whole business is very unfair," she said. "I really think I ought to speak to Mr Barnard."

Dan shook his head at once. "No, Mum, please," he begged. "There's no point." He sighed. "Besides, he's already said that if there's any more trouble, he'll drop me from the school team."

"Well, if you insist," Ann Legg agreed reluctantly. "But Julia will have a word with him, I'm sure." Julia Browne, Zak's mum, was a teacher at Muddington Primary.

"She won't," Dan said. "Zak's asked her not to."

After tea, Dan went round to the Brownes' to see his cousin. Sam, meanwhile, decided to call up Archie. It was his duty to sort things out, she reckoned. If he was such a genius then he ought to do something to prove it, not skulk away inside that old pig's bladder that he inhabited.

"Archie!" she wailed, gently rubbing the football. "Arise, O Archie!"

But nothing happened.

She tried once more, with the same

result. Archie, it seemed, had not yet returned from his outing to school.

Before going to bed that evening, Sam made another attempt to summon Archie, but again without success. She looked anxiously at the old football in her hands. *I hope he knows the way back*, she thought. Then she wondered if ghosts could get lost. For an instant, she imagined herself putting up one of the notices that she'd seen on trees: *Missing, black and white kitten named Fluffykins.* Only her notice would read: *Missing, phantom footballer named Archie . . .* No one could see him, though, so they wouldn't be able to help find him, would they? She went to bed feeling quite concerned about her ghostly relative.

Archie still hadn't returned next morning when Sam tried once more to summon him. She told Dan of his continued absence on the way to school.

"Oh, that's all we need," Dan groaned. "The day before our first ever cup match and our coach goes missing." He looked so glum that Sam decided not to mention her worries that Archie might actually be lost.

What seemed like further bad news awaited Dan on his arrival at school. He was to go at once to the office of Mrs Samuels, the head teacher. "What now?" he wailed.

"Perhaps she's heard what's happened to you and wants to talk about it," Sam suggested hopefully. Then, less hopefully, she added, "She might be on your side."

"Yeah, and pigs might fly," Dan muttered darkly.

He went off to his interview with a face like stewed rhubarb.

Yet when Sam next saw him, at morning break, he was grinning like Christmas Day! Beside him, Zak and Zoe were grinning too.

"What is it?" she cried, unable to believe her eyes. "What's happened?"

"It's all sorted!" Dan yelled and he gave his sister a great hug.

"Oi, you're crushing me!" Sam spluttered laughingly.

Dan released his grip and put his arms round Zak and Zoe. "We're go-o-ing to

Wembley. We're go-o-ing to Wembley," he crooned happily.

"You're going to Wembley?" Sam quizzed incredulously.

Dan laughed. "Well, we're going to Muddington Rovers against Tottenham anyway," he crowed. Then he explained how his fortunes had turned around so dramatically.

The summons to Mrs Samuels' office had not been to receive further bad news – quite the contrary. Mr Barnard had phoned in sick that morning. He'd sounded very shaky

indeed, the head teacher had said. However, he had been very concerned that a message should be given to Dan. It was this: Dan, Zak and Zoe were excused the school team trip the next day. Indeed it seemed likely that the whole trip would be cancelled, Mrs Samuels had said, for Mr Barnard had sounded in a terrible state.

"But can we go to the Muddington Rovers game on Sunday?" Dan had implored the head teacher anxiously.

"Yes, of course," Mrs Samuels had assured him. "Mr Barnard was quite particular about that. 'Tell them, I shall see them on Sunday,' he said." Then she had sent Dan back to his classroom.

"So that's it! Everything's going to be all right after all!" Dan rejoiced.

"Why do you think he changed his mind?" asked Zak.

"Who cares!" said Dan. He started singing again and, this time, Zak and Zoe joined in.

Sam watched them, a broad smile on her freckly face.

But then a dark cloud blotted her sunshine. Everything wasn't yet all right, was it? Archie! What had happened to Archie?

Chapter Nine

ARCHIE GOES A-HAUNTING

As it turned out, Sam need not have worried about Archie. Returning from school that afternoon, she, Dan and Zak immediately got out the old ball to call up their ghostly relative . . . and out he fizzed, glowing brighter than ever and looking extremely pleased with himself.

"Greetings, lads!" he declaimed heartily. "I take it that all is well."

"Archie!" Sam exclaimed. "Where on earth have you been?"

"I have been a-haunting," he replied

mysteriously. "But first, have you any news to tell me?"

Excitedly Dan told Archie all about his meeting with Mrs Samuels and the good tidings she had given him.

"I don't know what made old Barnard change his mind," Dan concluded with a shrug. "But he did, that's the important thing."

Archie's moustache waggled with amusement. "I think I might know what made Mr Barnard change his mind," he gloated.

The three children gazed hard at their phantom manager.

"Archie!" Sam cried. "It was you!"

"What did you do?" Dan enquired.

"I merely made your teacher see the error of his ways," Archie replied teasingly.

"Come on, Archie!" Sam urged. "Tell us what happened, please!"

"Very well," Archie intoned suavely. "Sit down and all shall be revealed."

There was nothing Archie liked better than relating a story to an attentive audience

– and no audience could have been more attentive than Sam, Zak and Dan. They listened, completely enthralled, as he told them of his exploits the evening before.

Having failed to make the desired impression on Mr Barnard at school, Archie had decided he would have to follow his fellow manager home and there indulge in some serious haunting. It wasn't something he'd done much of, he explained, which is why his efforts in the classroom had not been more successful.

"Once I entered your Mr Barnard's

house, however, I soon mastered the technique," he said proudly. "And then, though I say it myself, I was rather good."

Usually these statements of self-praise brought groans from the children, but on this occasion they were too eager to hear what Archie had to say to interrupt.

"I began with some simple tricks," Archie continued. "Mr Barnard hung up his coat. I knocked it off its peg and on to the floor. He picked it up, I knocked it off. And so it went on, up and down, for some minutes, until he became irritated and I grew bored. Then we went into the kitchen, where the real fun began." Archie paused, radiant at the memory. "I opened cupboard doors, he closed them. I opened them again. He closed them. I opened them – and so on. Then I chucked a few things about the room, as we ghosts are wont to do."

"What sort of things?" Dan asked, tugging on his ear.

"Oh, you know, rice, sugar, eggs, that sort of thing," Archie replied casually.

"Wow!" Sam exclaimed.

"Cool," said Zak.

"By now, he seemed a little perturbed," Archie continued, "but still not sufficiently agitated, I felt. So I emptied a bag of flour over his head."

"You emptied a bag of flour over Mr Barnard's head?" Dan gawked.

"Indeed I did," Archie nodded. "Just to let him know I was there, to get his attention."

"I bet you did that all right," laughed Sam.

Archie raised one bushy eyebrow. "It seemed to do the trick," he confirmed. "Then I delivered my message. It was the same one I had expressed in the classroom, but, one to one, its effect was considerably more powerful – particularly as I wrote it in the spilled flour." Archie beamed at his young relatives. "A nice touch, I thought," he added.

Archie had haunted Mr Barnard all night long. He had pursued him around the house, tripped him up and snatched things from his grasp. When the teacher had tried to hide in bed, Archie had tipped up the mattress and pulled the pillow out from beneath his head. And everywhere – in flour, in ink, even in the condensation on the windows – Archie had written his message: *Dan, Zak and Zoe must be allowed to play for Leggs United on Saturday without penalty. Signed, Archibald Legg, the Phantom of the Cup.*

"It seems to have got through to him, eventually," Archie concluded with a flourish of his walrus moustache.

"Archie, you're a genius," Dan declared exuberantly. "You really are."

"Laddy, laddy," Archie retorted nonchalantly, "tell me something I do not already know."

Chapter Ten

WRONG-FOOTED

Number 15 Poplar Street was a happy, noisy house on Saturday morning. There was a real buzz of excitement in anticipation of the weekend's cup games. Practising on their recorders, the twins even managed to play the same melody at the same time – and almost in tune. It seemed, to Sam and Dan, like a good omen for what was to come.

There was only one minor hiccup: the state of the meadow. The moles had been busy again during the night and there were a number of bumps on the pitch. Sam and

Dan discovered them when they went down for a kickabout after breakfast.

"If Archie sees these molehills, he'll do his nut," Dan remarked, with an anxious pull on his ear.

"You're telling me," Sam agreed, flicking back her fringe. "We'll just have to make sure he doesn't see them," she stated decisively.

"How are we going to do that?" Dan asked.

"Like this," Sam cried, and she leapt with both feet on to one of the molehills. Then she leapt again. "We'll flatten them," she laughed, stamping.

"I thought you liked moles," Dan teased.

"Well, I do," Sam declared. "But I don't want to play on a pitch covered in bumps. Anyway, we're not actually hurting the moles."

Dan followed his sister's lead and soon Zak and the twins appeared and joined in as well. Flattening the molehills turned into a fun game. The five children leapt about the meadow like giant, jet-powered frogs. It was tiring too. After a while, they all collapsed

in the middle of the pitch and lay on their backs in the late summer sunshine.

"That was cool," Zak commented and, noisily, the twins agreed.

"Good fitness training too," Dan observed breathlessly.

"And we got rid of all the bumps," Sam said contentedly.

Their efforts did not go unappreciated, when Archie inspected the pitch later, just before the kick-off against Amberley Park.

"There are a few blemishes, I see," he remarked with a slight twitch of his moustache. "But all in all, the surface seems to be in reasonable condition." He turned to his team with a serious expression. "I shall expect great football from you this afternoon," he said gravely. "Remember this is the cup. A draw is no use. To progress, we must win. Let's make this a memorable weekend: a victory for Leggs United in the cup today; a victory for Muddington Rovers tomorrow." He paused, before continuing in a lighter tone, "As the great Herbert Chapman once said, 'All good things come in twos.' "

The children laughed.

"You made that up," Dan accused the phantom footballer.

"Well, perhaps I did," Archie confessed and his eyebrows hopped playfully. "Still, it's rather good, don't you think?"

Dan and Sam looked at each other and groaned.

Amberley Park were a strong team. They were high in the league like Leggs United and had only lost once away from home. Watching them line up in their yellow and black striped shirts, Dan regretted all the training sessions his team had missed that week. He hoped they wouldn't be made to pay for their lack of preparation. In any case, he felt pretty sure he was in for another busy afternoon.

In fact, during the first half, both defences were busy. The match was end to end, one side attacking and then the other. The main threat posed by Amberley came from their right-winger, a tall, tricky player called Tom. A couple of times early in the game, he took on Justin and went past him on the outside. Fortunately for Leggs United, his crosses were not very accurate and were easily cleared. As the half went on, however, the winger changed his line of attack to come inside Justin on the defender's right foot, which was his weaker one by a long way.

The first time the Amberley winger adopted the tactic, he completely surprised Dan and his fellow defenders. Darting easily past Justin, Tom found himself in the Leggs United area with a clear run on goal.

He took full advantage. Sprinting forward, he slipped the ball past the advancing keeper, Gabby, into the bottom corner of the goal. Amberley Park were in the lead.

But their lead didn't last long. In keeping with the game so far, Leggs United went on the attack from the restart and forced a corner. Sam swung the ball in from the right with her left foot, Rollo Browne flicked the ball on at the near post and Zoe headed it into the top of the net. She lost her glasses in the process, but she didn't care. She stood in the Amberley goalmouth, grinning sort of woozily, until Zak returned her glasses. Then she ran back to her own half with her arms in the air, whooping like a hyena. It was her first ever goal for Leggs United.

On the touchline, Ann and Stephen Legg, Mark and Nadya Legg, and Julia and Otis Browne applauded wildly and shouted encouragement. Beside them, Archie allowed himself a small, indulgent smile, while his outline shone like polished silver.

It was Amberley Park and their winger,

Tom, who had the last laugh, though – at least in the first half. Only minutes after Zak had hit the inside of the visitors' post, the ball was played out to the Amberley right. Tom took the ball in his stride and ran at Justin. He dummied to go outside the full-back, then cut inside again. Justin was completely wrong-footed and, once more, Tom was through.

This time, though, Dan had got himself in a better position to cover the winger's run. However, he too was fooled by the winger's trickery. A clever shimmy and the Amberley player had another clear shooting chance. He arrowed the ball into the far corner of the net with Gabby helpless. Amberley Park were ahead again and Leggs United were in trouble.

Chapter Eleven

TWIN SWITCH

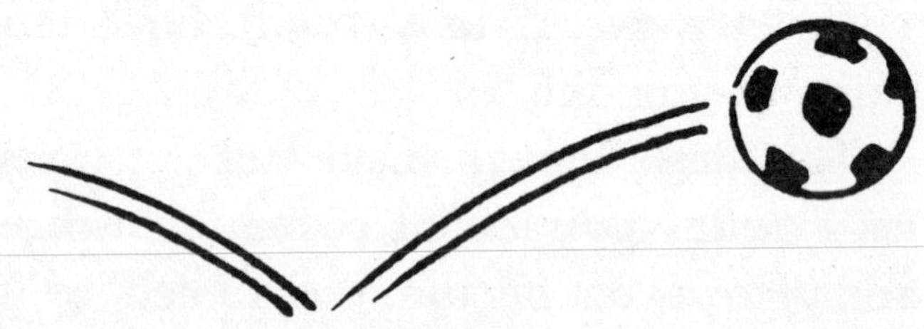

Leggs United were still two–one down when they came off at half-time. It had been an even game, though, and they weren't too disheartened. Nor indeed was Archie. He regarded his team thoughtfully.

"For the most part," he contended, "your play has been admirable." He gazed down at the diagram of Arsenal's famous ten-second wonder goal that was painted on the grass next to the pitch. "At least," he added, "your attacking play has been good. Defensively, we have a problem."

"That winger's brilliant," Dan declared.

"He's not bad," Archie conceded. "He reminds me a little of Cliff Bastin – very cool in front of goal." Cliff Bastin was a fast, goal-scoring winger in Herbert Chapman's Arsenal team. Archie had mentioned him many times and always with the greatest admiration.

"The thing is," Dan worried, "how are we going to stop him?"

"Yes," Sam agreed sharply. "It's no good us scoring goals at their end if he keeps scoring in our goal. We've got to do something." She tossed back her head impetuously.

Archie raised one large, pale hand. "Patience, patience," he soothed. "Am I not Archibald Legg, master tactician?"

"You mean you've got a solution?" Dan asked eagerly.

"Naturally," Archie replied. "For the second half, I intend to make a slight adjustment. The twins, Jules and Dustin–"

"Giles and Justin!" chorused the twins as one.

"Er, quite so," Archie blustered. "Giles

and Justin will switch sides – Giles on the left and Justin on the right."

His announcement was met with blank looks and bewilderment.

"Is that it?" Dan queried, bemused.

"That's it," Archie beamed. "A master-stroke, don't you think?"

The children glanced at one another and shrugged. What on earth was Archie up to?

The brilliance of Archie's plan, however, soon became apparent. In Amberley's first attack of the second half, the ball was quickly fed out to Tom. Without hesitation he ran at his opposing full-back, who was now the right-footed Giles, not the left-footed Justin. As in the first half, Tom feinted to go outside, then stepped inside. But this time, the winger was attacking the full-back's stronger side and Giles easily took the ball off him.

Minutes later, Tom got the ball again and attempted the same manoeuvre, a little quicker this time. But Giles made another strong tackle, winning the ball back for his team, who mounted an attack of their own.

As Leggs United went forward, Tom gazed at Giles with a puzzled expression. Dan could see what he was thinking: How could this full-back, who was so weak on his right foot in the first half, suddenly become so strong on that side now? Dan smiled. The winger obviously hadn't noticed that Leggs United were playing identical twins at full-back.

When, in the visitors' next attack, Giles robbed Tom for a third time with a fine right-footed tackle, the Amberley player shook his head and frowned. He looked completely disheartened. The next time he received the ball, he didn't attempt a run.

He just kicked it back into his own half.

With Tom shackled, Amberley's attacking options were severely weakened. At the other end of the pitch, meanwhile, Leggs United were rampant. On the wings, Frances and Ben, two of the Legg triplets, were causing havoc with their pace. The tiring Amberley full-backs were no match for them. So it was no surprise when, from one of Ben's runs, Zak hit the equalizing goal.

Now the second half became one-way traffic in the direction of the Amberley goal. Prompted by Sam's clever playmaking, Leggs United created several chances: Zak hit a post, Rollo had a shot cleared off the line, Sam herself curled a free-kick just over the bar. Finally, though, Amberley cracked.

It was a move that would have brought a smile to Herbert Chapman's face, as Archie remarked later. Dan won the ball deep in defence. He slid it through to Sam in midfield. She swivelled and swept the ball out to the left flank, halfway inside the Amberley half. Frances sprinted after it, carried the ball forward to the penalty area, before crossing to Zak. He controlled the ball and advanced in one movement, then flicked the ball inside to Ben who raced on to fire an unstoppable drive past the Amberley keeper. Leggs United were in the lead!

The Leggs spectators cheered and hugged one another. This time, even Archie showed his delight. He waved his arms in the air and did a little jig of joy, his knobbly knees pumping comically. Watching him, the twins collapsed in a fit of laughter.

For the rest of the game, Amberley were a beaten side. Their heads went down and they were no match for their exuberant opponents. Zak dribbled past three defenders to score his second goal and Sam completed the rout with a fine run and shot from the edge of the Amberley penalty box.

When the final whistle went, Leggs United had won by five goals to two. Their first ever cup match had ended in a great victory . . .

Now, it was over to Muddington Rovers.

Chapter Twelve
THE BIG MATCH

The atmosphere inside the ground was electric. At each end, rival supporters sang their chants lustily. There was a real sense of expectation amongst the Muddington Rovers crowd that today their team could pull off an amazing giant-killing feat and knock out the mighty Tottenham Hotspur.

In their special seats in the central stand, the Muddington Primary football team chattered excitedly, discussing their recent meeting with the Muddington Rovers players.

Dan gazed down in awe at his programme and the autographs he had collected. All the Muddington Rovers players had signed their names and so too had the Tottenham Hotspur stars. Beside Dan, Archie hovered restlessly in the aisle, looking around with interest and impatience, while in the seat on Dan's other side, Zak sat staring at the pitch, as if he were in a dream. It had all been so amazing.

One member of the party seemed particularly overawed by the occasion. It wasn't a child; it was Mr Barnard. He was very quiet all afternoon and appeared to be uncharacteristically nervous. He kept glancing over his shoulder as if he feared someone was following him – and with some justification, for every now and then Archie did indeed take up a position behind the teacher, looming over him like an avenging angel. Once the phantom footballer even proposed pouring a cup of cold tea over the teacher's head, but Dan dissuaded him.

"I think you've haunted him enough,

Archie," he said firmly. "He's got the message."

"Oh, very well," Archie muttered disappointedly. "I must say I was rather enjoying being a troublesome spook."

"Well, now you can be a spooktator instead," Zak joked.

As they waited for the teams to appear, Archie entertained his young relatives with talk of famous cup upsets of the past – the greatest of which involved Herbert Chapman's Arsenal.

"It was just a year before he died, 1933," Archie stated solemnly. "The press called Arsenal 'The Bank of England', because of all their expensive players, while Walsall, their opponents, were worth just £69. Several influential Arsenal players were unable to play, however, having been laid low with influenza." Archie sighed deeply. "Sadly, their replacements were not up to the mark," he lamented. "Walsall won by two goals to nil."

Archie's expression was so tragic that Dan felt quite sorry for him.

"Oh well," he cajoled. "If the great Arsenal can be beaten like that, then there's hope for Muddington Rovers, isn't there?"

This suggestion appeared to revive Archie's spirits. "You have a point," he conceded, with a small twitch of his big moustache.

As it happened, however, the game began badly for Muddington Rovers. Tottenham Hotspur took the lead with their first attack of the game and, by half-time, they were three goals ahead.

During the interval, Archie decided to join Stephen Legg, Sam and the twins, who were watching the match from behind one of the goals.

"It's good to get an all-round view of the game," he declared coolly, before floating away through the air.

"I bet Sam's in a right strop," Dan remarked, watching Archie go. "Tommy Banks has hardly had a kick."

"Except that one the Tottenham sweeper gave him," observed Zak ruefully.

Dan tugged at his ear anxiously. "He'd

better not get injured," he said. "It would ruin our surprise."

His worries, however, were unfounded. The second half was far more evenly balanced than the first and Tommy Banks played as well as anyone. In fact, to the home crowd's delight, he scored the only goal of the half. With just minutes remaining, he jinked past two Tottenham defenders and thumped the ball into the net. It may only have been a consolation

goal, but the Muddington supporters celebrated as if it were the winner.

At the end of the match, the Muddington Rovers team was given a standing ovation by their fans – Dan, Zak and Zoe among them. The applause continued until the last player had left the pitch.

And then, as the spectators started to leave, came the tannoy's announcement.

Chapter Thirteen

A SPECIAL SURPRISE

"Will Sam Legg please see the steward at Entrance P. He has an important message for her." The announcement resounded around the emptying stadium.

Sam sat bolt upright in her seat with a look of astonishment on her freckly, now pink face. Beside her, hovering in the aisle, Archie raised one bushy eyebrow.

"That's you, Sam!" cried the twins as one.

"It is," Stephen Legg agreed. He looked at his daughter with a wry smile. "Unless there's someone else in this ground with exactly the same name," he teased, "which I doubt very much."

"But what can it be about?" Sam wondered. She peered across at the special area of the central stand where Dan, Zak, Zoe and the rest of the Muddington Primary school team had been seated. But the seats were empty.

"Don't you think you ought to go and find out?" Stephen Legg prompted.

"Go on, Sam!" Justin shouted.

"Hurry up!" Giles urged.

"An excellent idea," Archie agreed. He wrinkled his moustache theatrically. "I shall accompany you."

Entrance P was just above them and, as most of the spectators in their block had departed by now, it took Archie and an excited Sam only moments to get there.

"Sam Legg?" enquired a burly man in a luminous yellow steward's jacket.

Sam nodded. "Yes," she said breathlessly.

"I'm to take you to your brother," the steward informed her. "He needs to speak to you about something."

"What is it?" Sam asked, puzzled.

"I don't know, love," the steward shrugged. "I'm just the messenger."

Sam turned to her ghostly relative. "Come on, Archie!" she urged.

"Eh?" said the steward in obvious confusion.

"Oh, nothing," said Sam quickly, blushing. "I was just talking to my invisible friend."

"Ah," said the steward with an understanding smile. "I used to have one of them. Bobo, I called him."

"Bobo!" Archie repeated disdainfully, as he followed Sam and the steward out of the stand.

They walked along several corridors and down a number of staircases before stopping at last by a door that said: *Private – Hospitality Suite.*

"Well, here we are," the steward said genially.

Sam's heart was racing as the steward opened the door. But it almost galloped away completely when she saw who was in the room beyond, looking straight at her as she walked through the doorway. It was Tommy Banks! Next to him, with a huge grin on his round face, was Dan.

"Surprise, surprise," he grinned.

"Ah, this must be my number one fan," Tommy Banks greeted Sam. "Put it there." He reached out a hand to shake. "It's a pleasure to meet you," he said warmly.

For once, Sam was quite lost for words. She just nodded her head with a shy smile and shook her hero's hand.

"Your brother tells me you wanted my autograph, so I've signed this for you,"

said Tommy Banks. He handed Sam a programme of that day's match against Tottenham. Across the front, he'd written: *To Sam, best wishes. Thanks for your support!* Then he'd signed his name underneath.

"Thanks," Sam muttered, quite overcome.

Tommy Banks winked. "It's the least I could do," he remarked. "Sorry we couldn't manage a win for you."

"That's OK," Sam uttered timidly.

"Well, you can't win 'em all, can you?" Tommy Banks continued heartily. "Unless you're Man. United, of course." He grinned broadly. "Well, I'd better get back to the bath," he laughed, "before the lads take all the hot water." He put his hand on Sam's shoulder for a second, then winked again. "See you. Keep cheering," he said. Then with a quick wave of his hand, he strode away.

Sam watched her hero go, then turned and threw her arms round Dan's neck.

"You're a star," she cried happily.

"It was Tommy Banks's idea," Dan said

modestly. "When I told him how much you adore him, he said he just had to meet you."

Sam snorted.

"He seems a nice enough young fellow," Archie remarked amiably. "Though I still say he could do with losing a few pounds. Now, in my day . . ."

"Oh, Archie, be quiet," Dan said good-humouredly. "Can't you see Sam's in love?"

Sam aimed a playful punch at her brother.

"Hmph," said Archie, his eyebrows hopping like frisky caterpillars. "It takes all sorts, I suppose." He stroked his moustache thoughtfully. "Well, Muddington Rovers may have lost a game, but they've certainly won a heart." He nodded at the still beaming Sam – and, in that joyful moment, the phantom manager shone like the FA Cup itself.

Spot the Ball

For Richard, my oldest pal,
goalie turned playmaker

Chapter One

ASK ARCHIE

"It's there!" Sam Legg exclaimed. "It's got to be there."

She was leaning over the competition page in her brother Dan's football magazine, pointing to an area in the picture where she thought the invisible ball should be. The competition was called *Spot the Ball* and showed two players jumping in the air. The ball had been removed from the picture and you had to guess where you thought it should be.

"No, you're wrong," said Dan, shaking his head. "The ball's over here." He pointed to a spot at the other side of the picture.

Sam Legg tossed back her fringe dismissively. "Don't be stupid," she snorted. "They'd have to have their heads on back-to-front for the ball to end up there."

Dan eyed his sister coolly. "Since when were you such an expert on heading the ball?" he demanded. Then, with a sniff, he added, "Your heading's about as good as your tackling."

Sam Legg made no secret of the fact that she found tackling boring. *She* liked passing, dribbling and shooting – and hardly ever tackled at all. She was the midfield playmaker of Leggs United, the family football team that she and Dan played in. Dan was the team's central defender and captain. He was a strong tackler and, having the advantage of being tall and well-built, was good in the air too. Though only a year younger than her brother, Sam was a good foot shorter and not noted for her heading ability.

"You don't have to be brilliant in the air to know that the ball can't be where you say it is," Sam retorted tartly, ignoring her brother's jibe about her tackling. "You won't win this competition and get those cool yellow boots if you put your cross there." A dreamy look came into her eyes. "I want a pair of red boots like Tommy Banks wears," she sighed. Tommy Banks was the star of the local league club, Muddington Rovers, and was Sam's favourite player. She had pictures of him all over her bedroom wall.

"Well, I won't win with your suggestion," Dan insisted. He frowned thoughtfully for a moment or two. "I've got an idea," he said suddenly. "Why don't we ask Archie what he thinks?" Archie, alias Archibald Legg, was the children's great-great-uncle and the manager of Leggs United. He was also a ghost.

Sam's green eyes narrowed, as she considered her brother's suggestion. Then she nodded. "OK," she agreed. "But I bet I'm right."

They went over to a glass cabinet that stood against a wall near the door. Inside was an ancient brown leather football, flanked by an equally aged pair of bulky shin-guards. On top of the cabinet was an old black and white photo of Archie himself, dressed in football kit.

Sam opened the cabinet and took out the football. For over sixty years, since he had been struck down by lightning during a match, Archie had inhabited the old ball. For most of that time, the ball had lain flat and forgotten in the Leggs' loft with Archie trapped inside. It was only recently that the ball had been discovered and Archie released.

Rubbing the ball gently, Sam spoke the words that had magically brought forth her phantom relative, like the genie from Aladdin's lamp, on that first occasion and on many others since. "Arise, O Archie!" she wailed. "Archie, arise!"

There was a fizz and a flash like a firework rocket igniting and out of the ball flared Archibald Legg. He was dressed, as ever, in the full kit (though a very old-fashioned one) of Muddington Rovers, for whom he had played during his lifetime. He wore a black and green striped shirt, long, baggy white shorts and green woolly socks that concealed thick shin-pads. On his feet were clumpy leather football boots with gleaming steel toe-caps; at his throat, worn cowboy-style, was a red neckerchief, whose brightness contrasted with the ghostly pallor of his skin. Most impressive of all, though, was his facial hair: an enormous walrus moustache; vivid, bushy caterpillar eyebrows; and a flaming red mane that stood up on his head as if he was permanently in the grip of an electric shock. Around him a ghostly aura glowed.

"Right, gather round, gather round," he commanded grandly, his eyes looking up towards the ceiling. "It is time I commenced my pre-match address . . ." He waggled his huge moustache imperiously and prepared to continue.

A loud cough from Sam stopped him. He looked down at her with a deep frown that drew his eyebrows into a hairy V.

"Yes?" he enquired testily. "What is the matter, laddy?"

Dan grinned at his ghostly ancestor. "It's not match time yet, Archie," he said with a chuckle. "We're still at home."

Archie looked about the room with a confused air. "Then why have you summoned me?" he demanded at last.

"We need your help," Sam said with a wrinkle of her small, freckly nose.

"Yes, your expert opinion," Dan added flatteringly – and with immediate effect. Archie's frown changed at once to a beaming smile. He positively shone.

"Ah, yes, of course," he murmured warmly, "I'm always happy to impart my considerable expertise. What is it? A tricky tactical problem? A question of strategy? A move requiring that little touch of brilliance that only I can supply?"

Dan and Sam looked at one another and rolled their eyes.

"It's nothing like that," Dan muttered.

"No, it's this," said Sam, thrusting the magazine page in front of Archie's startled gaze. "We want you to tell us where in the picture you think the missing ball should be. I think it should be here . . ." she pointed at her chosen spot, "and Dan, huh . . ." she laughed in ridicule, "well, he thinks it should

be there!" She spoke as if her brother's suggestion was the most absurd she had ever heard in her life.

Archie took hold of the magazine and stared at it quizzically for some seconds. Then he regarded his young relatives with cool disdain. "You are both quite wrong," he announced. "The ball is obviously here." He indicated a spot on the ground, almost directly underneath the leaping players.

"How can that be?" Dan queried, pulling at one ear with a perplexed expression.

"Yes, how can you be so sure?" Sam asked suspiciously.

"Ah," sighed Archie smugly. "Call it ghost's intuition." He tapped one bony finger on his long nose and his smile grew even more radiant. "Or, I suppose, you could always call it genius . . ."

Chapter Two

MIXED FRUIT

A couple of hours later, the Leggs United players were in Drayton Park, standing in a tight group as Archie began the team talk he'd been about to give in the sitting room earlier. At the other end of the pitch, their opponents, St Luke's Boys' Club, were gathered in their own little huddle.

"Now, lads," said Archie with an indulgent wiggle of his moustache, "this match today is the first of two successive away fixtures – St Luke's today and, er . . ." He hesitated for a moment, frowning vaguely. "Well, some other team next week," he concluded fuzzily.

"These matches, I am sure, will be the biggest test of your progress so far. Any reasonable side should win their home games; it is getting results away that distinguishes a really good team."

Archie paused to study his players for an instant, before continuing, "When Arsenal first won the championship under Herbert Chapman in 1931, they collected half of their points *away from home*, scoring a record 60 goals." These words were accompanied by the expression of deep reverence that always appeared on Archie's face when he mentioned the great Arsenal manager and his team.

"Of course," he added, "their fast, counter-attacking style was perfectly suited to playing away. They soaked up pressure and then, suddenly, broke free like rampaging lions. Desperate defence became deadly attack in seconds. That is how I expect you to play this afternoon – and next week too. Banana, raspberry, satsuma, prickly pear, kumquat . . ."

The children stared at Archie in astonishment. Dan and Sam's younger brothers, the

twins Giles and Justin, fell against each other, laughing.

"Prickly pear!" cried Giles.

"Kumquat!" giggled Justin.

"Archie, what are you talking about?" Dan quizzed his phantom relative.

Archie seemed momentarily as bemused as his team. "How curious," he said at last. "I suddenly heard this spirit voice in the air, listing fruit. There must be a greengrocer haunting nearby."

Sam shivered. "Not too near, I hope," she said, glancing warily about her as if trying to spot the phantom.

"Yeah, supposing St Luke's have got a ghost too," said Zak.

But Archie wagged his head. "Huh," he snorted. "I don't think the ghost of a greengrocer is worth worrying about. He would hardly be a match for the great Archibald Legg."

"Except at taking *banana* shots," quipped Dan.

"And making *grape* saves," joked Zak.

Archie glowered at his young relatives, but before he could make any retort, the referee blew his whistle for the teams to get ready for the kick-off. Leggs United lined up in their normal WM formation, a system invented by Herbert Chapman.

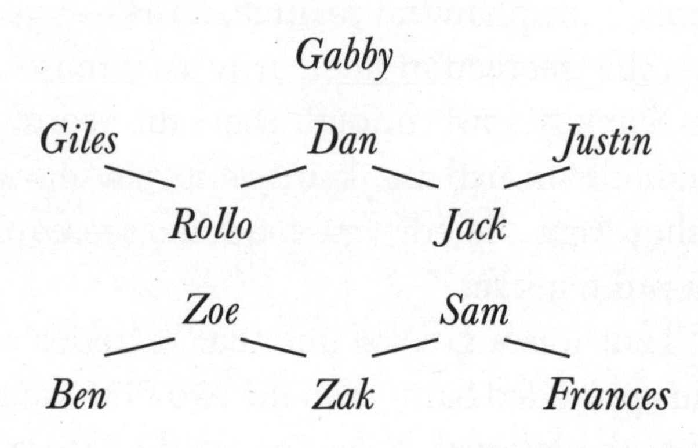

Archie took up his customary match position near the halfway line, standing with his hands on his hips and with one foot on the old ball. Further along the touchline was a small group of Leggs United supporters: Stephen Legg, his brother Mark, and their sister, Julia Browne. The Leggs United team was made up from the children of these three siblings.

"Come on, you Leggs!" Stephen Legg shouted, as the referee blew his whistle for the game to begin.

It was, as Archie had predicted, a stern test for Leggs United. St Luke's Boys' Club were a strong team with some skilful players. They were very sporting too – unlike some of the sides Leggs United had met in the League – and the game was played in a competitive, but friendly spirit. At half-time, the score was nil–nil; Sam had been closest to scoring with a shot from the edge of the penalty area that shaved the bar.

"That was a great shot," the St Luke's captain applauded Sam when the two sides walked off at the interval. "You deserved to score."

"Thanks," Sam replied with a freckly smile. "I'll aim a little lower next time."

Archie was happy enough with his team's first-half performance. They just needed to add a little more pace to their counter-attacks, he said, and he drew their attention, as he often had, to Arsenal's famous ten-second wonder goal, a diagram of which was whitewashed on the grass beside their home pitch, The Meadow.

"Strike quickly, that's the secret," he proclaimed.

Five minutes into the second half, Leggs United had the perfect opportunity to follow their manager's instruction. They'd been under heavy pressure for the whole of those five minutes and St Luke's had forced a couple of corners in succession. From the second one, the ball broke to Sam who was standing just outside her own penalty area. Finding herself in space, she sprinted forward to the halfway line, then slid the ball beyond the last St Luke's defender and into the path of Zak. In a couple of strides he was inside the St Luke's penalty box and, as the goalie came out, he calmly slotted the ball into the bottom left-hand corner of the net.

"Great goal, Zak," Dan congratulated his cousin and best friend, as he ran back to the centre circle. He grinned. "It was a real *peach*, in fact," he said.

Archie certainly looked well satisfied with his team's efforts. He waggled his moustache flamboyantly and glowed like an electric fire. However, the glow faded to a flicker when, a little later, a mix-up in the Leggs defence let in the St Luke's skipper to score the equalizer. As the ball trickled over the line, Archie put one transparently pale hand over his eyes and sighed.

The match continued to be hard-fought with both teams having dangerous attacks. Rollo Browne, Zak's older brother, had a header cleared off the line and Zak himself went close too. At the Leggs end, Zak's younger sister Gabby was in spectacular form. As well being a goalie, she was an excellent gymnast and it showed in her keeping. She wasn't very big, but she had a

terrific leap. Twice she soared like a swallow to tip goalbound efforts over the bar.

"That was brilliant," said the St Luke's captain admiringly the second time. "I was sure that shot was going in." Gabby just smiled shyly, as she got to her feet.

Dan played his part too. He tackled superbly and, as the game neared its end, kept encouraging his tiring team-mates.

With five minutes left, Leggs United were awarded a free kick on the left-hand side of the St Luke's penalty area. Dan sprinted upfield to join the attack.

"Cross it in, Sam!" he urged, as he passed his sister to take up his position near the opponents' goal.

Sam stood over the ball, surveying the crowded penalty box. She tossed back her fringe, then trotted towards the ball purposefully, eyes gazing forward. At the last moment, though, instead of crossing the ball, she flicked it sideways towards her cousin, Ben Browne.

For an instant, the players in the penalty area were completely dumbfounded. They stood staring out at Sam, as if searching for the ball. In that instant, Ben had sprinted forward to the byline. Glancing up, he whipped a low cross into the six-yard box straight to the feet of his cousin Zak. A second later, the ball was nestling in the St Luke's net.

"Goal!" The three Leggs United parents jumped up and down in excited celebration. Beside them, Archie's glow returned. There was nothing he liked better than a piece of quick thinking, especially when it resulted in a goal for his side.

"Lemons," he murmured, repeating the ghostly whisper he'd just heard in the air. He shook his head and sighed. "Greengrocers!" he said to himself. "They have no appreciation of great football . . ."

Chapter Three
NUTS

Zak's goal proved to be the winner. A few minutes later, the referee blew his whistle for the end of the match.

"Three cheers for Leggs United!" cried the St Luke's skipper.

"Hip, hip, hooray!" his team responded three times.

"Three cheers for St Luke's," Dan replied, returning the home team's gesture.

The players shook hands as they walked from the field.

Archie greeted his team with a huge, hairy smile. "An excellent contest," he purred.

"Played in the true spirit of the game." His moustache twitched contentedly.

"You think Herbert Chapman would have approved, then?" Dan remarked, a big smile on his round face.

"Undoubtedly so," Archie agreed happily. He turned to Sam Legg. "And that free kick was worthy of the wee wizard, Alex James, himself," he declared with an appreciative wag of his large head. "It reminded me of the goal he scored to win the 1930 Cup Final against Huddersfield Town."

Sam grinned. She knew this was praise indeed, for the Arsenal playmaker Alex James was Archie's favourite player. "Not bad for a girl, eh?" she observed teasingly.

Archie fixed Sam with a steely gaze. "You're all lads to me," he retorted. He looked around his players proudly. "My lads, my team, my coconuts." His eyebrows hopped like startled caterpillars. "Coconuts?" he repeated questioningly.

"It must be that ghostly greengrocer again," laughed Dan.

"Mmm," Archie muttered disapprovingly.

"Well, I wish he would keep his talk of fruit to himself. This is a playing field, not a shop." He glanced about him with a stern expression. Then his face relaxed once more. "Anyway, that was a fine performance," he said warmly. "Although there are one or two things I should like to put straight before the next match . . ."

"That win puts us above the Colts in the table now," said Zak Browne, who loved football statistics of all kinds.

"Yes!" Dan shouted joyfully, punching the air. The Muddington Colts were the team that Perry Nolan, Dan's arch-enemy, played for. They were also the next team due to visit Leggs United's home ground, The Meadow, in two weeks' time. The sides had met once before, in a summer tournament, when Leggs United had won narrowly. "We're going to thrash them at our place!" Dan crowed and he jigged with delight.

Archie yawned and his outline started to glimmer weakly, like a torch with a fading battery. "All this excitement has made me quite weary," he said woozily. "I think it's

time I retired to my pig's bladder for a rest. Please do not disturb me until the morning." So saying, he began to disappear from the children's sight. Within seconds, he had dematerialized into the old ball, the inner part of which was, indeed, made of a pig's bladder.

The twins came running over. "Hey, Dad says he'll buy us all an ice lolly if we hurry up and get changed!" cried Giles.

"Yeah, we can have any flavour we like!" Justin whooped. "Orange, banana, strawberry . . ."

"Sounds like Dad's heard that ghostly greengrocer too," Dan said happily to Sam and Zak. He looked up into the sky with his arms held aloft. "Goodbye, Mr Greengrocer, whoever you are!" he proclaimed dramatically.

"You're crazy," said Sam, wrinkling her nose.

"Nuts," added Zak laughingly.

Dan lowered his arms and picked up the old ball. "Come on, let's go and get changed," he said. "I want my Strawberry Sparkle." He ran off towards the changing pavilion, closely followed by the rest of the team.

Chapter Four

LOST BALL

On Sunday morning, Dan was lying in bed, happily reliving some of his best moments from the previous afternoon's game, when the door to his room suddenly flew open and Sam burst in. Her freckly face was pink with emotion.

"Dan!" she cried breathlessly. "What have you done with the ball?"

"Eh? What ball?" Dan questioned sleepily.

"Archie's ball, of course!" Sam hissed sharply. "It's not in the cabinet. Where did you put it?"

Dan frowned. "What do you mean, where

did I put it? I didn't put it anywhere," he replied, bemused. "I thought you had it," he added tentatively, tugging on one ear.

"Of course I don't!" Sam snorted fiercely. "I wouldn't be asking you if I did, would I?"

Dan shrugged. "Dad must have it, then," he said coolly, but he felt a small ripple of unease.

"I'll go and ask him," said Sam, rushing out again.

Dan quickly leapt out of bed and followed his sister.

Stephen Legg was in the kitchen, eating toast and reading his newspaper. He looked up in mild amusement as Sam and Dan rushed in.

"There's no hurry," he remarked amiably. "The breakfast bar's still open." He brushed a few crumbs from his beard.

"Dad, where's Archie's ball?" Sam demanded. "It's not in the cabinet."

Stephen Legg pulled an extravagant *search me* face. "I've no idea," he said. "Have you asked your mother?"

But Ann Legg hadn't seen the ball. Neither

had the twins, Giles and Justin. Subsequent enquiries to the Legg family next door and the Brownes down the street also drew a blank. Nobody, it seemed, knew where the old ball was.

Dan peered at the glass cabinet in the sitting room, where the ball was usually kept. The old leather shin-guards were there, but there was a space where the ball should have been. Who had had the ball last, he wondered? He'd carried it to the changing room, he remembered that.

Then they'd all gone off to have an ice cream . . .

"Sam, Sam!" he shouted, his face flushed with panic.

"What is it?" Sam asked anxiously.

"I think the ball's still in the changing room!" Dan cried. "Let's get Dad. We've got to go and get it back!"

Fifteen minutes later, Stephen Legg drove into Drayton Park, the home ground of St Luke's Boys' Club, with two highly agitated young passengers, Dan and Sam. Also in the car was Zak Browne, who very rarely got worked up about anything. But even he was looking concerned. Without the ball, they couldn't summon their phantom manager. If the ball was lost, so was Archie.

The moment the car drew to a halt, the children had their doors open and were racing towards the pavilion. Once inside they rushed to the changing room they'd occupied the day before . . .

Their spirits sank as they looked around the empty room. They searched under the benches, but there was nothing there.

"It's gone," said Dan glumly. He sat down on one of the benches with his head in his hands.

"Maybe someone handed it in," Zak suggested brightly. "Or maybe the janitor found it."

"Yeah, let's ask at the office," said Sam decisively.

They knocked on a door marked *Park Superintendent.* A plump, elderly man wearing glasses and a green uniform answered. "Yes?" he wheezed.

"We've lost a ball," Sam gabbled.

"What's that?" queried the man, frowning. "Lost Abel? Who's that? Your dog? Your brother?"

Sam shook her head vigorously. "No, not our dog. We've lost our *ball*!" she said emphatically.

"It's a special ball," Dan added. "It's very old and it's . . ." He was about to say the ball was magic – which was true, of course – but he suddenly thought it would sound stupid to say so. "It's very heavy," he continued, "and made of worn, brown leather."

"Sounds like you could do with a new one," the man suggested. He prodded his glasses higher on his nose. "I've got a couple in lost property that no one's claimed . . ."

"We don't want a new ball!" Dan exclaimed. "We want our old one back."

"We left it here yesterday afternoon," Zak explained.

"Could you have a look in lost property for us?" Sam pleaded.

The park superintendent coughed and patted his chest. "Well, yes, I suppose so," he said genially. He disappeared inside his office for a moment and then reappeared with a huge bunch of keys. "Follow me, lads," he instructed.

He led Dan, Sam and Zak along the corridor to a door with the words *Lost Property* painted on it and a heavy padlock on its handle. "Now," he said, peering through his glasses at the mass of keys, "which of these is the right one, I wonder?"

Waiting for the park superintendent to locate the padlock key was agony for the children – especially Dan, who tugged anxiously at one ear, then the other and, finally, both at once.

"Ah, here we are," said the superintendent at last. He put the key in the padlock and the bolt clicked free. Then he pulled the door open. "See if you can find your ball in there," he urged, standing aside.

Eagerly the children rushed into the room, rummaging through a motley assortment of muddy socks, boots, jerseys, gloves, scarves, shin-pads, tennis balls . . . They found a bicycle pump, a notebook, a dictionary, two flat footballs – but not their ball, not Archie's ball.

"It isn't here," said Dan disconsolately.

"No," Sam agreed, equally distressed.

"Is there anywhere else it could be?" Zak asked in desperation.

"Well," sighed the superintendent, "the janitor's the man to ask. He may have put your ball somewhere, I suppose."

As one, the three children gazed up at him with revived expectation.

"Where can we find him?" Dan asked excitedly, infused with new hope.

But the superintendent's frown was not encouraging. "Ah, that's the problem, you see," he said with an apologetic shake of his head. "Right now he's on a plane to Ibiza." Then, taking in the children's dumb bewilderment, he explained, "He's gone to Spain for his holidays. He left this morning."

"When will he be back?" Dan enquired weakly, hope suddenly sliding down into his shoes.

The superintendent looked bleak. "Not for a fortnight, I'm afraid," he said grimly.

Chapter Five

MISSING ARCHIE

Dan was inconsolable. It was all his fault the ball was lost. He was the one who'd left it in the changing room – and all because he'd been too busy thinking about ice cream. Now poor Archie was doomed to spend the rest of his ghostly existence – or at the very least the next two weeks – trapped inside the old ball.

"I'm sure it'll turn up," Ann Legg tried to reassure her oldest son, but without success.

Stephen Legg contacted the St Luke's Boys' Club to see if they had the ball or knew where it might be, but they didn't. They said they'd look out for it next time they played. The park superintendent was very helpful too; he put up a notice about the missing ball in the Drayton Park pavilion. But it seemed to Dan and the rest of the Leggs family that the best – perhaps only – hope of finding the ball lay with the absent janitor. How on earth would they be able to bear the next fortnight?

An atmosphere of profound gloom descended on the homes of the Leggs and Brownes over the next days. They had grown very fond of their ghostly relative and his funny ways, since the day Sam and Dan had first summoned him from the old ball. Already they missed his stories about Herbert Chapman and Arsenal; they missed his colourful training sessions and his extraordinary ball skills; they even missed his boasts about what a genius he was.

"If only Archie would turn up, he could claim he was the greatest manager in the entire universe ever and I wouldn't care," sighed Sam sadly the next afternoon when she and Dan and Zak were in the meadow doing some half-hearted practice.

"Nor would I," Dan agreed. Archie did like to blow his own trumpet, it was true, but he was amazing. His tactics were brilliant. They may sometimes have appeared bizarre, but they always proved successful in the end. He was the one who'd formed the team in the first place. How could it go on without him, Dan wondered.

"Do you think we should cancel Saturday's match against Limpton Park?" he said to the others.

"I don't know," Sam said, wrinkling her small nose. "I don't feel much like playing."

"No," Zak concurred. He peered out glumly from behind a line of drooping black ringlets. "It won't be the same without Archie."

The three sat in melancholy silence for a minute or so, then Zak said, "But I think Archie would want us to play. Remember what he said on Saturday about good teams being the ones that did well away from home. He thought this game was really important."

"Yes, you're right," Dan agreed. He saw a

picture in his head of Archie shimmering and flickering before them, outraged at the idea that they might not play. Sam had a similar vision.

"Yeah, he'd want us to play all right," she nodded.

"I guess we ought to carry on then," said Dan, though he didn't sound very enthusiastic.

At that moment a horn honked at the other side of the meadow. Looking up, Dan groaned. Perry Nolan was there on his bike, leaning on the fence and looking smugger than ever.

"I hear you lost your lucky ball. Shame," he jeered.

"How do you know about our ball?" Dan snapped.

Perry shrugged. "I saw the notice, didn't I?" he said. "Down at the park."

"Yeah, well, we don't need your sympathy," Dan added roughly. "So you can clear off."

Perry laughed unpleasantly. "Well, you'd better find that lucky ball before you play us next week," he said, "cos you're going to need all the luck you can get."

"You're the ones who'll need luck," said Sam, tossing her head defiantly. "We'll murder you."

"Yeah," Dan said. Then he smiled slyly. "Have you looked at the league table recently?" he enquired with pretend innocence.

Perry scowled. "You've just been lucky so far," he snorted. "Wait till you play some decent opposition. We're going to take you apart."

"What, like you did at your place?" Sam laughed, and Zak and Dan joined in.

"Four–three, four–three!" they chanted. That was the score Leggs United had won by when they'd played the Colts in the summer.

"You can laugh now," Perry sniped. "But you won't be laughing next week. We want revenge – and we're going to get it, whether you've got your stupid ball or not!"

With this heated prediction, he hooted his horn loudly and rode away.

Chapter Six

SPOT THE PROBLEM

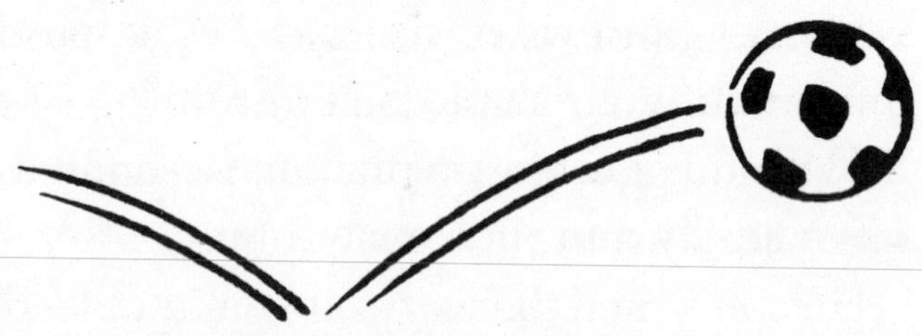

If losing Archie wasn't catastrophe enough, the following morning brought a new disaster: chickenpox!

It wasn't Dan himself who was infected – all of his family had had the illness. So had their cousins next door. But Zak hadn't.

Rollo Browne, Zak's older brother (who had had chickenpox as a baby), broke the news on his way to school.

"Zak's got chickenpox," he announced in his usual understated way. "He's covered in spots."

"Oh no, poor Zak," said Dan sympathetically. Then a thought occurred to him. "He'll be OK for Saturday, won't he?" he enquired.

"Of course he won't!" Ann Legg exclaimed. "He can't go anywhere till those spots go."

"How long will that take?" Dan asked with an anxious pull of his ear.

"A week or two, I think," his mother informed him. "Your dad's the one to ask." Stephen Legg was a doctor. Dan quickly went off to seek his professional opinion.

He confirmed the worst. It would indeed be about a fortnight before Zak would be able to play for Leggs United in a match again.

"I suppose Billy will have to play against Limpton Park," Dan said. Billy was Zoe and the triplets' younger brother.

"Well, Billy's a good player," said Stephen Legg encouragingly. "And he's been to most of Archie's training sessions, hasn't he?"

"Yes," Dan agreed gloomily.

"Well, then," Stephen Legg continued heartily. "Cometh the hour, cometh the man, as they say. I'm sure Billy will do just fine."

"Mmm," Dan muttered without conviction.

Billy *was* a good player for his age, but losing Zak was a big blow. He was Leggs United's top goalscorer and his goals – like the two against St Luke's the previous Saturday – had regularly won or saved games for the team. They couldn't expect Billy to do that. He'd never played a proper football match in his life.

Dan went round to see his sick cousin when he got home from school that afternoon. Zak was tucked up on the sofa in the Brownes'

living room, watching a video of his favourite programme, *The X Files.* As Rollo had said, Zak was very spotty and his face was a bit swollen. He looked a bit like something out of *The X Files* himself, Dan thought – but he didn't say it. He said how sorry he was that Zak was ill, then he talked with his friend about the team situation.

"I guess you could play Rollo up front," Zak suggested. Rollo was the oldest and tallest of the cousins and once or twice in the past Archie had played him as a striker.

"Yeah, I suppose so," Dan agreed. "He's not as good as you, though."

"He's good in the air," said Zak, trying to be positive.

"Mmm," Dan muttered uncertainly. He pulled at his ear. "You've got to play in the Colts match, though," he declared desperately. "Even if you have to wear a mask or something."

Zak smiled. "I'll be OK by then," he said confidently.

Dan looked at his friend questioningly. "Do

those spots hurt?" he asked. He'd been really young when he'd had chickenpox and he couldn't remember anything about it.

"Not really," Zak shrugged. "They're just itchy, that's all. Mum puts this white cream on my skin to stop them itching so much. But I still want to scratch them."

Dan nodded. The two sat in thoughtful silence for a moment or two, then Dan said, "I wonder why it's called chickenpox? I mean, you don't look like a chicken, do you? More like a Dalmatian."

"Yeah," said Zak with a wistful glance at his spotty arm.

At that instant something green and slimy squelched across the TV screen.

"I didn't know Perry Nolan was on *The X Files*," Dan joked grimly and Zak laughed.

His laughter quickly died, though, when the door opened and Gabby came into the room. Dan stared at her, horrified.

"Oh no!" he cried. "Not you as well!"

Gabby wasn't as spotty as her brother, but she bore the tell-tale marks of chickenpox. Her skin was lighter than Zak's and her spots were more prominent. They stood out on her face like bumpy red ink blots.

"They've just appeared," said Gabby. "Max has got them too." Max was Zak and Gabby's little brother.

"This is a disaster," groaned Dan. "What are we going to do now? We won't have a full team on Saturday – we'll have to play with ten men."

"But who'll play in goal?" Gabby asked anxiously.

Dan sighed helplessly. "I don't know," he said. He put his head in his hands. "Everything's going wrong," he moaned, shaking his head miserably. "If only Archie were here . . ."

Chapter Seven

THE GOBBLER STRIKES

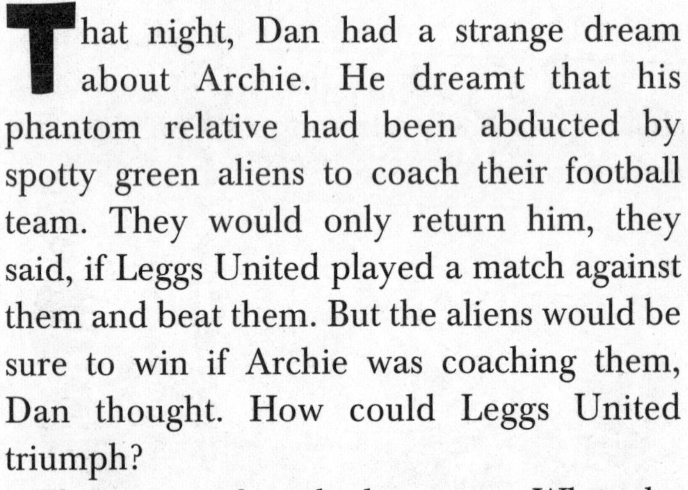

That night, Dan had a strange dream about Archie. He dreamt that his phantom relative had been abducted by spotty green aliens to coach their football team. They would only return him, they said, if Leggs United played a match against them and beat them. But the aliens would be sure to win if Archie was coaching them, Dan thought. How could Leggs United triumph?

Things went from bad to worse. When the aliens lined up, there were hundreds of them and when Dan looked around he saw that the rest of his team had disappeared: he was all alone. And there, on the touchline, was Archie, standing as usual with his hands on his hips. But the old ball had turned into a coconut, Archie's hair, eyebrows and moustache had gone green, and his face was all spotty!

"Oh no," Dan groaned, as he realized that Archie had become an alien. Now they'd never get him back; Archie was lost for ever . . .

Dan woke up soaked in sweat. He'd had scarier nightmares before, but none that left him feeling so awful. He told Sam about the dream at breakfast. But her response wasn't very sympathetic.

"You *should* feel bad," she said bluntly, with a toss of her head. "It's your fault that Archie's lost."

"But I didn't do it on purpose," Dan protested.

"It doesn't make any difference, does it?" Sam persisted, but then seeing the hurt look on her brother's face, she softened a little and added, "We'll just have to do our best until Archie turns up again, won't we? Even if we have only got ten players."

"Yeah," Dan agreed. He tried to sound positive, but it wasn't easy when he still had a ghastly picture of a green-haired, spotty Archie in his head.

"I think we ought to have a team meeting," Sam continued. "We need to get things sorted for Saturday – like who's going to play in goal."

Dan nodded. "Yeah, you're right," he said

with an air of resignation. "Let's get everyone round tonight."

It was a long day. Dan found it difficult to concentrate at school, with everything that was on his mind. Several times he was told off for daydreaming.

"Is there something bothering you, Daniel?" asked his teacher, Mrs Williams, at the end of the afternoon.

"Ah, no, I'm just a bit tired," Dan replied, faking a yawn.

"Well, I hope you'll be a bit more awake tomorrow," said his teacher. "You looked like you were on another planet today."

"Yes, sorry, Mrs Williams," Dan apologized. His teacher didn't know how right she was, he thought.

That evening, at the team meeting, another problem emerged: two of the triplets, Ben and Frances, had had an argument and neither turned up. The other triplet, Jack, reported what had happened.

Both Ben and Frances had bought goldfish at the weekend, he said. Ben had bought a big

goldfish that he'd called The Gobbler, while Frances had got a smaller fish that she'd named Michael Owen, after the Liverpool striker.

"Michael Owen?" Dan queried. "Why did she call it Michael Owen?"

"She said it moved really fast like Michael Owen," Jack said. "And anyway, she likes Michael Owen."

"Huh," Sam snorted, flicking back her fringe fiercely. "Tommy Banks is better than Michael Owen any day."

"Yeah, we know you love Tommy Banks," sighed Dan. "But we still don't know what's up with Ben and Frances."

All eyes turned to the oldest of the triplets again. Small spots of pink appeared on his pale cheeks and his blue eyes were bright with the importance of his news.

"Well, the thing is," he continued animatedly, "that when we came down to breakfast this morning, there was only one goldfish in the bowl." He paused and raised his hand dramatically. "It seems like The Gobbler ate Michael Owen!"

This news, tragic as it may have been for the consumed goldfish's owner, reduced the twins to a fit of giggles.

"The Gobbler ate Michael Owen!" squealed Giles.

"Gobble, gobble, gobble!" cried Justin, demonstrating how he thought the dirty deed had been done.

"It's not funny, though," said Jack. "Frances is really upset. She said Ben's fish was a disgusting cannibal and Ben said her fish was stupid and he was glad The Gobbler had eaten it. And now they're not talking to each other."

Dan frowned and shook his head. "So now we're down to eight players," he said bitterly, "and all because of a couple of goldfish." He sighed deeply. "Let's hope they make up by Saturday."

"At least they'll be on opposite sides of the pitch," remarked the triplets' older sister, Zoe.

"Yeah," Dan agreed wearily. "But will they both be on *our* side?"

Another matter was concerning Sam. "We still haven't decided who's going to take Gabby's place in goal," she reminded her brother.

"I don't mind playing in goal," shrugged Rollo.

"No, we need you up front, Rollo," Dan said firmly.

"I'll play in goal!" cried Giles and Justin at the same time.

"You can't *both* play in goal," said Sam.

"I'll be goalie first half," said Giles.

"And I'll be goalie second half," added Justin.

"No one'll beat us," Giles declared confidently.

"No way!" Justin affirmed.

The two boys each mimed a spectacular dive, tumbling into each other and collapsing noisily on the floor.

Dan raised his eyes to the ceiling and sighed.

Chapter Eight

A CHAPTER OF ERRORS

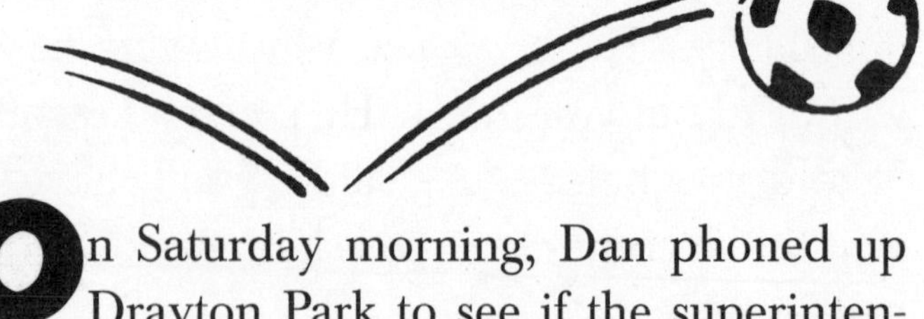

On Saturday morning, Dan phoned up Drayton Park to see if the superintendent had any news about their ball. It was a long shot, he knew, and he wasn't at all surprised to be told that the ball still hadn't been found.

"We've had a card from the janitor, though," said the superintendent cheerfully and Dan's spirits rose a little.

"What did he say?" he asked, pressing the receiver tighter to his ear.

"Well," the superintendent continued wheezily, "he says he's having a wonderful time: the sun's been shining every day and the swimming pool's lovely. Yesterday, he went on a coach trip to an old monastery and had his feet washed. But he doesn't think much of the food."

"But what about the ball?" Dan interrupted impatiently. "What does he say about our ball?"

"Your ball?" the superintendent muttered quizzically. "He's in Ibiza. Why would he be writing about your ball?" He coughed raspily. "I told you before," he said, "you'll have to wait till he comes back to ask him about your ball."

Dan sighed. "OK," he said. "But what day *does* he come back exactly?"

"Hmm, I'm not sure," breathed the superintendent. "Sunday, I think."

"Are you sure it's not Saturday?" Dan gasped pleadingly. He couldn't bear the thought of Archie missing Leggs United's match against the Colts. That was a game they absolutely had to win.

"Maybe," said the superintendent vaguely. "All I know is, he'll be back next weekend. I suggest you phone again then."

"OK, thanks," Dan said with a gloomy air.

There was no time to dwell on this latest setback, for there was the match against Limpton to think about. The good news was that Ben and Frances were both going to play (their parents had insisted); the bad news was that they still hadn't made up. The twins had offered Frances one of their stick insects as a substitute for her gobbled goldfish, but she'd declined. A stick insect wasn't a real pet like a goldfish was, she'd remarked huffily.

The feud between Ben and Frances seemed to affect the whole team. There was an uneasy, tetchy atmosphere among the Leggs United players as they gathered on the pitch that afternoon. It wasn't the easiest of circumstances in which to give a first ever team talk, but Dan did his best.

"OK, everyone," he said with a heartiness he didn't actually feel, "let's put all our problems behind us and really go for it. If Archie was here he'd probably tell us some inspiring story about Herbert Chapman and Arsenal, but all I can say is that we're going to have to try twice as hard as normal to make up for being a player short. It's going to be tough – but we can do it, can't we?"

The response was not the rousing chorus he'd hoped for; more a muted selection of mumbles and grunts. But at least it was a generally approving response. No one told him to shut up or go and stick his head in a bucket. However, later that afternoon, that was just about what he felt like doing.

At first, things went OK for Leggs United. Their ten players matched the eleven of Limpton with admirable skill and determination. As Dan had urged, the team put in a sterling effort. In midfield and defence, they chased and harried and denied the Limpton players space. Billy ran his heart out and even Sam made a few tackles, which was almost unheard of.

Up front, though, Ben and Frances were definitely not on their game. They stood out on their wings, as far apart as possible, almost hugging the touchlines on either side of the pitch. When Sam tried to bring her cousins into play by hitting passes over the top of the

Limpton defence for them to run on to, she got only a half-hearted response. The two wingers, who were usually so quick, trotted forward lethargically and failed to get to a single pass.

For nearly half an hour of the match, Leggs United held firm and actually looked the more dangerous of the two sides. But then things suddenly started to go badly wrong.

The first Limpton goal came as the result of an awful mistake. A lucky ricochet off a Limpton player sent the ball spinning into the Leggs United half, where it dropped into the path of their central striker. Even so, there should have been no problem, for he was a long way from the Leggs United goal and still had Dan to get past. As it happened, though, he didn't even attempt to do that. Instead, he looked up, and then lofted the ball high in the air towards the goal.

Dan turned untroubled, expecting to see Giles collect the ball and kick it back upfield. But what he actually saw, to his horror, was Giles upside down doing a handstand!

"Giles!" he screamed. "Look out!" But his

cry came too late and had the opposite effect he'd intended. Instead of springing up to save the ball, Giles tumbled and sprawled face down in the mud, raising his head, just in time to watch the ball bounce by him into the unguarded net. Limpton were in the lead.

Five minutes later, they got a second – and this time it was Dan himself who scored it! Jumping to head the ball away from a corner, he mistimed his leap and the ball banged against the back of his head and flew into his own net. Giles didn't have a chance. It was Limpton two, Leggs United nil.

Worse was to follow in the second half. First, Justin somehow managed to let a gentle shot roll between his legs to give Limpton their third goal and then he and Giles collided in the penalty box to allow the Limpton central striker to score easily into an empty net. As if this wasn't disaster enough, Zoe tripped and twisted her ankle and Leggs United had to play the last ten minutes with only nine players – and one of those, Billy, was so exhausted he could barely stand up. It was amazing that they managed to keep the score to just four–nil. Even so, it was easily the worst defeat Leggs United had ever suffered.

Trudging off at the end, the Leggs players looked utterly dejected. On the touchline, their parents were equally sombre and subdued. The contrast in mood from the previous Saturday was enormous.

The last to leave the field, Dan had the longest face of all. What would Archie have said, he thought, if he'd seen his team play so badly? He pictured the phantom footballer alight with outrage. But then, he reflected, if

Archie had been there, Leggs United wouldn't have lost as they had. He would have come up with a plan to save the game, wouldn't he? He always did. They needed Archie. Oh, where was Archie?

Chapter Nine
DOWN AND UP

The more he thought about it, the more Dan was sure that he was to blame for the state Leggs United were in. After all, he was the one who had lost the ball in the first place. Then as captain he had failed to lift his team when it had mattered. He'd even contributed to their defeat by scoring an own goal. That Sunday morning he was feeling about as low as could be.

"I think perhaps someone else should take over as captain," he suggested defeatedly to Sam at breakfast that morning.

Sam wrinkled her nose thoughtfully. "You

can't give up now," she said with a decisive shake of her head. "Archie chose you as captain; you've got to go on." Her green eyes narrowed with determination. "Archie will be back soon and then everything will be fine," she added hopefully.

Dan didn't look convinced. "But what if the janitor doesn't know where the ball is? What if Archie really is lost?" he said miserably, tugging at his ear.

Sam shrugged. "I don't know," she replied grimly. "All we can do is hope and do our best."

Sam's positive words failed to lift her brother's spirits. He gazed into his cereal bowl as if it was a deep black hole that might, at any moment, suck him in.

"Look, why don't we go down to the meadow for a quick kick-about," Sam proposed. "We need to get out of the house."

"Yeah, OK," Dan agreed wearily. He didn't really feel like playing football, but it was a more appealing prospect than moping around the house all day.

They walked down the garden to the fence

at the bottom, Sam leading. Dan was still climbing over when he saw his sister jolt to a stop.

"Hey! Look at that!" Sam shouted. She pointed across at the fence on the opposite of the meadow. Standing beside her now, Dan followed her finger and gasped. The fence was covered in graffiti.

LEGGS UNITED ARE RUBBISH
4–0! 4–0!

had been sprayed untidily across the wood in huge chunky letters.

Dan stared irately at the graffiti.

"Who could have done that?" Sam cried perplexedly.

But Dan knew at once who was responsible. "It was Perry," he declared angrily. "I know it was. He must have found out about our defeat and come down here last night to rub it in. I bet his stupid brother helped him." A picture came into his head of George and Perry Nolan sniggering as they scrawled their mocking message.

Dan's hackles rose. Gloomy resignation

had been replaced now by resentment and a burning desire for revenge. “We’re not going to let them get away with this!” he hissed.

“We’ll get our own back on Saturday,” Sam said fiercely.

Dan nodded. His hands bunched into fists as he glared at the graffiti. “First, though, we’ve got to get rid of this rubbish,” he growled. “No one’s ruining our ground.”

“No,” Sam agreed. She thought for a moment, then said, “Let’s go and ask Otis the best way to get it cleaned up. He’ll know.” They sprinted off to speak to Zak’s dad.

It was Zak himself who answered the door.

“Hi!” he said cheerfully.

“Oh, hi, Zak,” said Dan.

Sam said nothing. Her face froze in shock, as she took in the puffy blisters on Zak’s skin.

“You look awful,” Sam said at last.

“Oh no,” said Zak easily. “I’m getting better. Mum says. She reckons I’ll be fine to play on Saturday.”

“But what about those things on your face?” Sam persisted.

"You get these near the end," Zak assured her. "When the red spots have gone."

"That's great," Dan enthused, grateful for any good news. "What about Gabby?" he added tentatively.

Zak frowned. "She's still covered in red spots," he said grimly.

"Oh," sighed Dan. At least Zak would be back, though, he thought, as they went to find Zak's dad.

Otis advised them to paint over the graffiti. They'd never scrub it off, he said. He gave them two pots of paint and some brushes.

"Good luck, guys," he said.

Zak went with Sam and Dan, and the three of them spent the rest of the morning painting. It was hard work, but when they'd finished, the fence looked smart and clean and there was no sign of the graffiti.

They sat down for a while and admired their work in silence. Sitting between Sam and Zak, Dan felt a sudden rush of happiness at having his best friend around again. Things finally seemed to be looking

up – though there were still problems to sort out.

"We've got to get Ben and Frances to make up," he said at last.

"Yeah," Sam agreed. "But how?"

"If only Archie were here," Zak mused wistfully. "He'd find a way."

Zak was right, Dan thought. Archie would have found a solution. But Archie wasn't here, so it was up to him as captain to sort things out.

After a bit, he said, "I think I might have an idea." The others looked at him keenly.

"You know Frances really likes Michael Owen," he ventured.

"Yes," snorted Sam dismissively.

"Well there's a big pull-out poster of him in the middle of my magazine," Dan went on. "Supposing I give it to Ben to give to Frances. Like a kind of peace offering."

"Mmm, it might work," said Zak uncertainly.

"I think we should try," said Sam, tossing her head decisively.

As it happened, Ben was quite happy to go along with Dan's scheme. A week had gone by since his falling-out with Frances and he had no wish for the feud to continue. Frances too was tired of the situation and she accepted happily the olive branch of the poster. She didn't say so to Ben, but she actually preferred the poster to her goldfish. She put the picture of Michael Owen up on her wall next to a pop star poster that Zoe had given her.

"You know, Dan, that was a really good idea," Sam congratulated her brother later.

"Thanks," Dan said contentedly.

"In fact," Sam added, "it was a touch of genius – as Archie would probably say."

And the two of them laughed. Finally, it seemed, Leggs United were getting back on their feet again.

Chapter Ten

TWICE THE TEAM

The next few days were good ones for Dan and Leggs United. Hard on the heels of Ben and Frances's reconciliation came the good news that Zoe's ankle had fully recovered and she'd be OK to play against the Colts. The following day, a spotless Zak reported fit too. The only doubt now hung over Gabby.

Her spots had moved from the red to the blistery stage, but it was touch and go whether they'd all have scabbed over and gone by Saturday.

Dan thought it was important for team

morale that Gabby should come to the training session he'd called for Friday afternoon. But Zak seemed doubtful whether she would.

"She's really upset about how she looks," he warned his best friend. "Since she got chickenpox, she hasn't gone out at all. She says she looks like a monster."

"Mmm," muttered Dan and his brow creased in thought. "You've got to get her to come." Suddenly, his face lit up. "Tell her we've got a special surprise for her!" he exclaimed.

"What surprise?" Zak asked, puzzled.

"Well, you'll see," said Dan mysteriously and he tapped a finger to his nose in an Archie-like gesture.

Gabby took some cajoling, but Zak did eventually manage to persuade her to accompany him to the meadow that afternoon. She appeared dressed in a hooded top tied tightly at the neck so that little more than her eyes were visible. But they bulged with astonishment at the sight that confronted them. The faces of every single member of the team were covered in spots!

"Eh?" said Gabby, gaping at her team-mates in utter amazement.

Zak too was shocked. "Wh-what's going on?" he queried anxiously.

Dan licked his finger and smudged one of the spots into a blob. "It's OK," he laughed. "It's only felt-tip, see. I thought it would make Gabby feel better if we were all spotty too."

Gabby shook her head and grinned. Then, throwing back her hood, she joined in with the others. She very quickly seemed to forget

about her chickenpox, as she dived and leapt and twisted. In fact, as Dan noticed happily, she hardly had any spots now at all.

It was a very successful training session. Not that anything brilliant was taught or learned, as it probably would have if Archie had been in charge. But the team spirit was excellent. For just about the first time since losing their manager, the Leggs United players laughed together. They were a real team once more.

Spirits were still high next afternoon when Dan prepared to give his second ever team talk. Gabby's presence – now spotless like her brother and raring to go – was a massive boost. The twins' goalkeeping against Limpton had been eccentric to say the least; in Gabby, the Muddington Colts would meet a much surer and more formidable barrier.

Dan began his talk by reminding everyone of Perry Nolan's graffiti attack on the Meadow. Then he recalled the previous match between the two teams in the summer when Perry and his dad, Holt Nolan, who'd refereed that day, had tried to cheat Leggs United out of a deserved victory.

He didn't really need to say any more – everyone was really up for this game, he could tell. Somehow, though, it didn't feel like a proper team talk if there was no mention of Herbert Chapman or Arsenal. As he stood there, he recalled something Archie had once told him.

He drew himself up, Archie-like. "As the great Herbert Chapman once said of the Arsenal centre-back Herbie Roberts," he declaimed grandly, " 'There goes two players.' Well, I say that about Zak and Gabby." He paused dramatically.

"But they are two players," Sam pointed out.

"Yes, well," Dan mumbled, "you know what I mean. Last week, without Zak and Gabby, we were badly beaten. Today, with them, we will be twice the team – and the Colts won't stand a chance."

This time his statement was met by a loud whoop of appreciation.

"Right, let's get out and play," Dan urged.

*

Leggs United were warming up in the meadow when the Muddington Colts arrived. They drew up in two flashy limousines, provided by Holt Nolan, who liked to show how rich he was.

There was a cocky air about the visitors as they walked into the Leggs United ground. Perry Nolan strode in as if he owned the place and cast a quick smirking glance across at the fence where the graffiti had been.

"Found your ball yet, then?" he jibed as the referee called Dan forward for the toss-up.

"No," Dan hissed fiercely. "But we don't need it – not against you lot."

"Huh," sneered Perry. "We'll see, won't we?"

As the two teams lined up for the kick-off, Dan could feel the bond of determination and family pride that ran through his team. They might be missing their coach, but they were certainly not lacking spirit.

From the start, Muddington Colts were pushed back in their own half as Leggs United swept forward. Only stout resistance by George Nolan and his fellow defenders kept the home side at bay. Perry Nolan, as usual, did nothing to help his defence. While Leggs United attacked, he just hung about in the Leggs half waiting for someone to pass to him, so that he could grab the glory. For most of the first half, he was little more than a spectator.

When Zak scored with a scorching volley, it seemed like the Colts would be totally overwhelmed. But somehow they held out and, when the ref's whistle blew for half-time, the score was still one–nil.

Dan was a little disappointed that Leggs United's pressure hadn't brought more goals, but he was pleased with the way the team had performed. "Well played, everyone!" he congratulated his fellow players as they walked towards the touchline.

The next instant, though, it was something off the pitch that took his attention – a voice shouting. He turned to see a man coming through the gateway into the Meadow. The man was large and bald-headed with a deep tan.

"Are you Leggs United?" he asked.

"Yeah, that's us," said Dan with a tug of his ear.

"Ah, good," the man sighed. He put down the big canvas bag he was carrying and took out . . . an old leather football! "I believe this is yours," he said.

Chapter Eleven

A TRIUMPHANT RETURN

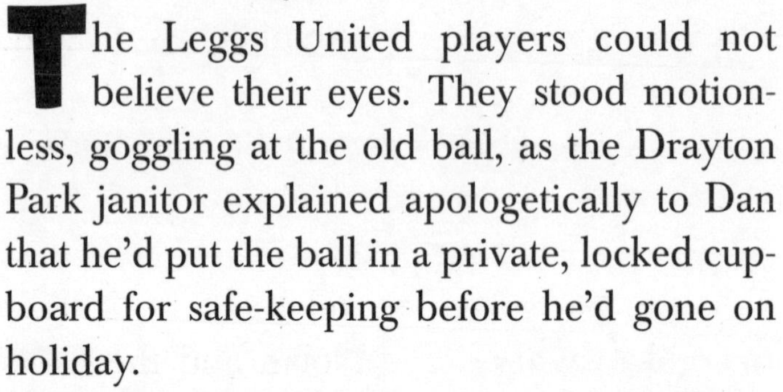

The Leggs United players could not believe their eyes. They stood motionless, goggling at the old ball, as the Drayton Park janitor explained apologetically to Dan that he'd put the ball in a private, locked cupboard for safe-keeping before he'd gone on holiday.

"I could see it was no ordinary ball," he said, looking at the ancient football affectionately. "They don't make them like this any more." He handed the ball over to Dan.

"Thanks," Dan said quietly, still stunned with surprise.

"No problem," the janitor replied with a smile. "Anyway, I'd best be off now back to the park. Good luck with your game."

"Yes, thanks," Dan said again. Then, as the janitor hurried away to the gate, Dan turned round and, smiling broadly now, held the ball aloft.

At once, his fellow players started shouting and racing across the pitch towards him. The adult Leggs joined the stampede.

Sam was the first to reach Dan. Without hesitation she grabbed the ball and began to rub it gently. "Arise, O Archie!" she wailed. "Archie, arise!"

And there, fizzing out of the ball like an electrified genie, was Archie!

"Free at last!" he exclaimed. He glanced around his gathered relatives and then beyond to where Holt Nolan and the Colts were looking on with a mixture of surprise and ridicule. All they could see was the old ball, because Archie was only visible to his family.

Archie's eyes flickered and glowered. "I see we are entertaining that team of petty chisellers," he said fiercely. "I trust we are winning."

"We are, one–nil," Dan nodded.

"Ah, excellent," Archie purred and his hairy caterpillar eyebrows twitched in a funny sort of dance.

Everyone wanted to know what had happened to the phantom manager. How had he spent the last fortnight? Archie held up his bony hands to demand silence.

"There is very little to tell," he proclaimed with a waggle of his moustache. "All I can say is how wonderful it is to be out in the real world again after spending two weeks inside a pig's bladder with that wretched greengrocer whispering in my ear about the price of cauliflowers and how many King Edward potatoes you get to the pound." He breathed deeply. "Now," he boomed. "I think you had better inform me of what I have missed."

Quickly Dan, with help from the others, sketched in the events of the past fortnight, concluding with the first half of the match against the Colts. Archie tutted at the

Limpton result and his outline flared with outrage at the news of Perry Nolan's graffiti attack, but his face relaxed into a smile as he heard about the team's recovery.

"When Herbert Chapman died in January 1933, his team experienced a similar collapse," Archie reflected soberly. "Top of the league at the time, Arsenal suffered three consecutive defeats. But like you, they recovered. Indeed, they went on to win the title for a third successive year." He paused a moment and regarded his team fondly. "I am proud of you all," he declared, his face beaming.

At that moment, the referee's whistle blew to summon the players for the second half.

"Is there anything you want to say to us?" Dan asked eagerly.

But Archie shook his large head. "You seem to be doing fine already," he replied warmly. "Just go out and play."

If Leggs United were good in the first half, in the second they were irrepressible. Archie's re-appearance inspired them to new heights of performance. The passing was crisper, the moves more pacy and imaginative, the effort even greater. Muddington Colts were pressed back once more.

Strangely, though, it was the away team who scored first. A long clearance found Matt Blake, who cleverly put Perry Nolan in on goal, one on one with the keeper. A brilliant diving save by Gabby denied Perry, but the ball fell to Matt, who slammed home the rebound. Perry Nolan celebrated like it was the winning goal in the cup final.

"I told you you were rubbish," he taunted Dan.

Dan ignored Perry, but inside he was seething. On the touchline, Archie was glowing like a Guy Fawkes bonfire, but, like his captain, he said nothing. He stood with one foot on the old ball, arms folded, glaring.

Leggs United played like a team possessed now, running their opponents ragged. It seemed only a matter of time before they'd get another chance to score. And so it turned out. Just minutes after Muddington Colts scored their equalizer, Zak latched on to a fine through-ball from Sam to fire the home team ahead again. Moments later, Zak repaid the compliment, laying the ball back for Sam to run on to and smash an unstoppable shot past the keeper. Leggs were three–one up!

The barrage continued. Ben hit the bar, Frances had a hard shot turned over by the goalkeeper, Zak put a couple of shots just wide . . . At the heart of the Colts' defence, George Nolan was looking more and more agitated. When Leggs United won a corner near the end of the match, he finally turned on his younger brother.

"Perry!" he screamed. "Get back here, you lazy lump, and help us out!"

Sulkily, Perry trotted back into his own penalty area and stood in front of Dan, not attempting to mark him properly.

Sam took the corner. It was a wicked inswinger, curling in from the right towards the centre of the goal where Dan was already leaping. He leant forward to head the ball, but it never reached him; Perry put up a hand and flicked the ball away.

The referee's whistle blew immediately.

"Penalty!" he said and he pointed to the spot.

"Referee!" Perry protested, arms raised in innocence. But no one supported him. George Nolan swore and shoved him angrily towards the edge of the penalty area.

Sam placed the ball on the penalty spot as if to take the kick, but instead, she turned to Dan. "It's all yours, bro," she said matter-of-factly.

"Me?" Dan queried. "But I'm a defender. I'm no good at penalties."

Sam shrugged. "It doesn't matter. We're going to beat them anyway." She walked away towards the penalty D. "Good luck," she called over her shoulder.

Dan took a deep breath, then he too walked to the edge of the penalty area. Sam was right, he thought; they were going to win whether he scored or not. But how sweet it would be to score a penalty given away by Perry! It would be the best revenge of all. Glancing across at Archie, he received a curt nod of encouragement. Then he turned back to face the goal.

The whistle peeped. Dan took a small hop then sprinted forward. He didn't quite connect with the ball as cleanly as he'd have liked, but it didn't matter. The ball skidded into the right-hand corner of the goal with the keeper going the other way.

As the ball hit the back of the net, Dan raised his head and his hands in jubilation. He'd scored! Leggs United had won! And, best of all, their phantom manager was back!

Chapter Twelve
NEW BOOTS

"There's a parcel for you," Ann Legg informed Dan when he came down to breakfast on Monday morning. "The postman just delivered it."

"For me?" Dan said, bemused. "Whatever can it be?" He only got parcels on his birthday and it was a long time till then.

"Let's go and see!" Sam exclaimed excitedly. She leapt up from the table and ran out into the hall. Dan followed her.

The package was on the hall table. It was quite a large box, covered in brown paper.

Sam picked it up and thrust it at her still dozy brother.

"Open it, then!" she urged.

Dan tugged at the paper, ripping it open. An envelope fell out. But his eyes weren't really interested in that. What they were staring at was the box that he'd unwrapped. He knew what it contained from the picture on the side, but he couldn't believe it was true until he lifted the lid and saw what lay there: a pair of brand new, beautiful yellow football boots, nestling in tissue paper.

"Wow!" he cooed. "Wow!"

With trembling fingers he lifted out the boots and held them up for Sam to see.

"They're brilliant," Sam enthused. "Really cool."

Dan bent down and picked up the fallen letter. Opening it quickly, he read the brief note of congratulation.

"I've won the spot the ball competition," he said happily. "So Archie was right . . ."

"Let's go and tell him!" said Sam.

"Yeah – and show him my new boots," Dan added. They scuttled off to the sitting room, where the old ball was now back in its proper place in the glass cabinet. Sam took it out and summoned her ghostly relative.

Archie wasn't at all surprised at the children's news. In fact, he was a little put out that they should have doubted his solution.

"Sorry, Archie," Dan apologized. "It just seemed such an odd place for the ball to be, down under their feet, when they were jumping in the air."

"Ah," said Archie with a conceited wiggle of his moustache, "always expect the unexpected. That way you stay one step ahead."

"Well, I guess we can't all be geniuses like you," Sam said with a freckly grin.

"No, that's true," Archie agreed smugly. "One grapefruit in the family is probably enough." Sam and Dan sniggered. "I mean one *genius*," Archie swiftly corrected himself. "That infernal greengrocer has got me spouting all manner of nonsense."

"*Sprouting*, don't you mean?" Dan joked.

"Hmm, very amusing," Archie remarked tartly.

"But honestly, Archie, how did you know where the ball was?" Dan persisted.

Archie raised one bushy red eyebrow. "Ah, well, actually I saw it."

"You saw it!" Sam exclaimed.

"Yes, indeed," Archie nodded. "It's one of the gifts we spirits have. They removed the ball from the picture but I could still see it, glowing faintly – rather like a ghost, I suppose."

"So it wasn't genius after all," Sam remarked pointedly.

"Yes, well, not exactly," Archie hummed. He coughed and quickly changed the subject. "Now let's have a look at those new boots of yours," he said.

Dan handed the boots over. He hoped his ancient relative would like them, but he didn't really expect him to, because they were so different from Archie's own clumpy, brown, steel toe-capped pair. He was sure Archie wouldn't approve of the yellow. He was wrong, though. Archie sighed rapturously.

"When Herbert Chapman was a player, he wore yellow boots," he explained in a quiet, affectionate tone. "He was always ahead of his time."

"Tommy Banks wears *red* boots," said Sam dreamily.

"Yeah, so does Paddington Bear," Dan laughed.

Sam glared at him.

"Oh well," Archie murmured. "Yellow or red, I suppose there's one thing to be said for wearing colourful boots."

"What's that?" asked Dan and Sam together.

"Well," said Archie with a glowing smile, "you may lose the ball, but you'll never lose your feet!"

For younger readers

FOOTBALL FEVER

By Alan Durant

Illustrated by Kate Leake

He-hits-a-screamer-past-the-keeper-into-the-roof-of-the-net-what-a-goal!

William has caught football fever. His symptoms are so severe that his sister's afraid there's no cure. He eats, talks and dreams football, and he's driving his sister crazy!

Then one day William's dream comes true and Dad takes him to a football club for the first time. The match kicks off and the tension builds. The score is nil–nil and William has a ball.

Will he score and be a hero for the day?

And who'll be next to catch the football bug?!

By Sandy Ransford

You may have silky skills on the pitch,
but have you got what it takes to tackle this book?

Bursting with brilliant puzzles, clever crosswords and hilarious jokes, this is the perfect activity book for any true football fanatic.

How do ghost footballers keep fit?
With regular exorcise

Which football team never meets before matches?
Queen's Park Strangers

CAN WE HAVE OUR BALL BACK, PLEASE?

Football poems by Gareth Owen

A truly top-of-the-league collection of football poems!

Gareth Owen's lifelong love of football blazes through this stunning book of beautifully crafted poems. All the joy, sorrow and sheer fun of being a player and a fan can be found in this wonderfully funny and heartwarming collection.

Can We Have Our Ball Back, Please?

England gave football to the world
Who, now they've got the knack,
Play it better than we do
And won't let us have it back

PAUL STEWART & CHRIS RIDDELL

Billy Barnes has to share his bedroom with the Blobheads – and somehow keep them secret from his mum and dad.

Blobheads are weird purple aliens from the Planet Blob.

When Zerek, Kerek and Derek cry, 'Blobheads to the Rescue!' Billy knows that complete chaos is just around the corner. They're brave. They're determined. But the Blobheads are also utterly bonkers. And Derek's idea of a clever disguise is to turn into a fluffy blue kangaroo . . .